The
TURNKEY
of Highgate Cemetery

The TURNKEY

of Highgate Cemetery

Allison Rushby

CANDLEWICK PRESS

Copyright © 2017 by Allison Rushby

First U.S. edition 2018

Library of Congress Catalog Card Number pending
ISBN 978-0-7636-9685-6

18 19 20 21 22 23 LSC 10 9 8 7 6 5 4 3 2 1

Printed in Crawfordsville, IN, U.S.A.

This book was typeset in Centaur.

Candlewick Press
99 Dover Street
Somerville, Massachusetts 02144

visit us at www.candlewick.com

For Isabelle Rushby
10/17/1918–11/20/2014

who, like Grace,
lost her voice
for a while

Chapter 1

December 1940
In which Flossie has a visitor

F lossie lowered the book she was reading as she felt the girl awaken from rest and leave her grave.

Amelia Deering. Interred in London's famous Highgate Cemetery September 8, 1852. Cause of death: scarlet fever. Age: seven years. Five years younger than Flossie herself had been when she had died of rheumatic fever at the age of twelve.

Flossie could see Amelia's image in her mind's eye, just as she could see all those who were buried within the cemetery grounds. Amelia wore the most beautiful white lace dress, a light-blue sash tied around her waist. A matching blue ribbon held her long hair back.

As Amelia approached, Flossie thought about summoning her Advisor, Hazel, then decided not to. She could handle this on her own. She stood from her armchair and opened the door to her Turnkey's cottage, which existed only in the twilight world she now resided in.

"Hello, Amelia," Flossie said, beckoning her in.

Amelia inspected the small room, with its two large armchairs and threadbare rug upon the floor. She took a hesitant step inside.

"Did you want to sit down?" Flossie asked her.

Amelia shook her head.

Flossie closed the door behind them both, noting that Amelia seemed nervous, but not confused. Still, Flossie always found it was a good idea to check if her visitors knew exactly who she was.

"Now, you understand that I'm your Turnkey. It's my job to see that you're happily at rest." This was true. Flossie cared for everyone here at Highgate. Out of all the interred buried within it, the cemetery had chosen her for the task. She would be Turnkey until another was called upon. This could be hours, days, weeks, or even centuries away.

Highgate Cemetery was part of the Magnificent

Seven—the pet name for the seven huge cemeteries built on the outskirts of London in the 1830s and 1840s. There was Highgate, of course, as well as Abney Park, Kensal Green, West Norwood, Brompton, Nunhead, and Tower Hamlets. Some of the cemeteries were more well known than others. Highgate, for example, was famous for its extremely beautiful Egyptian-style architecture, which had been all the rage in Victorian times. Kensal Green was stately and garden-like and had been modeled on Paris's fashionable Père-Lachaise cemetery. The seven cemeteries, however, had been left to their own devices for decades and were now a mess of crumbling headstones, ivy, and tree roots.

"I know who you are," Amelia answered. "I know why you have that iron ring and key in your hand."

Flossie followed Amelia's eyes down to her own left hand and the iron ring she held within it, one ornate key hanging from it—the key to Highgate Cemetery's gates for the dead. Amelia offered her something, which Flossie took.

"Oh," she said.

It was a very old sort of photograph called a memento mori—a picture taken of someone after death for the family to keep and treasure. It seemed a horrible thing to want to have, but Flossie had seen pictures like these when she was alive, and her mother had explained to her that back in Victorian times it was very expensive to have your picture taken. A picture taken after death might be all a family would ever have to remember a person by. Flossie attempted to keep her expression even as her still heart broke. The image was of a lifeless Amelia, a number of dolls placed around her — obviously her favorites.

"I was hoping that I might have one of my dolls, please," Amelia asked, so politely that Flossie's heart broke all over again.

Flossie had no idea what to tell her. Eighty-eight years had passed and all of Amelia's dolls were surely long gone. But then she thought of something. She knew what she'd do.

"I've got an idea . . ." Flossie began, but her voice was immediately drowned out by the wail of the air-raid siren. She froze, imagining the scene playing out in the skies above. "You probably know the living are having a war," Flossie yelled. "A very noisy one." She expected Amelia knew — even when at rest, her interred had a basic understanding of what was going on within their immediate surroundings, and theirs had been bombed. They were aware, yet blissfully unaware, in their dreams. Flossie herself had been at rest for a short time before becoming the cemetery's Turnkey, and it *had* been just like a lovely dream. She remembered it well. She had been having a picnic on a grassy hill with her sister, Emmeline, and . . . she stopped herself as the siren bore into her thoughts.

Flossie and Amelia stood in silence, waiting for the all clear to sound. Maybe it had been a false alarm. But no, the siren continued to wail.

Flossie moved in closer to Amelia so she wouldn't have to yell. "Why don't you return to rest and I'll be back later. I've got to see how bad things are out there tonight, but I'm sure I'll be able to work something out about your doll, too."

"Oh, thank you!" Amelia's face lit up, and then she was gone from the cottage. That lovely, peaceful feeling of one of her interred returning to rest swept over Flossie.

She started toward the door.

Time to see what was going on out there this evening.

Chapter 2

In which Flossie assesses the damage

Flossie stood atop St. Paul's Cathedral and surveyed a burning London.

It was usually incredibly tranquil up here on the Golden Gallery—the circular walkway that was nestled on top of the cathedral's dome. Flossie adored the clear view of the river Thames stretching out before her and the feeling of floating above the busy city below. Tonight, however, a war raged all around and things were anything *but* tranquil. A battle was playing out in the skies above the city, aircraft shells bursting into brilliant explosions of bright white and searchlights roaming the sky. Below, flames licked at the streets and buildings, coloring the smoke-filled sky with various shades of pink. The barrage balloons bobbed around the heavens in order to stop low-flying aircraft. They were a surreal shade of salmon compared to their usual shiny silver.

There had been so much damage this evening. After leaving Amelia and Highgate, Flossie had stopped by several of the city's famous historic buildings. Westminster Abbey, the British Museum, the Tower of London—they'd all been hit. Standing on the Victoria Embankment, not another person in sight, she had wondered crossly at the horrible wastefulness of it all. The living cared so little for life. If only she could introduce them to the dead in her cemetery. They'd give so much for just five more minutes of what the living seemed to take for granted.

She had closed her eyes then and thought of St. Paul's. Not a second later, she had appeared there. This was something only Turnkeys could do. By simply bringing a place to mind, she could be there in an instant. Even the name of a location was enough to go by.

When Flossie had opened her eyes once more, she

had seen exactly what she'd hoped to see — St. Paul's standing tall, proud, and untouched. The building had been highlighted against the strangely lit sky, a beacon in the midst of adversity, determined and strong like the Londoners beneath her.

An aircraft shell exploded somewhere close behind the dome and Flossie jumped, bringing her iron-ringed hand to her chest. She might have died sixteen years ago and didn't need to worry about her weak heart any longer, but old habits were hard to break. Another explosion saw her swivel her head to the far right as an aircraft shell exploded far above with a boom.

She stilled.

There was a man standing in the alcove that led out onto the Golden Gallery's walkway. His attention was fixed on the explosion, which meant he hadn't seen her yet. At first she thought he was a fire watcher, stationed atop St. Paul's to protect it from burning. But, no, this man was a twilight visitor — a man of the dead, not the living — she could tell by his ashen hue. Everything was a muted shade in her world; it was how you could tell the living world from the world of the dead.

Flossie frowned as she took in his uniform, gray-green against the lit-up sky. It was cinched in at the waist by a leather belt with a silver clasp that matched his high black leather boots, the pants tucked into them. He had a long ceremonial sword at his side, and his torso was studded with medals. But it was the half view that Flossie had of his cap that took her nonexistent breath away. Because there, in the center of it, flashed something else made of silver—the *Totenkopf.* It was this that saw her face fall, because she knew what it was: the distinctive skull-and-crossbones symbol of the SS—probably the most feared organization in the Nazi regime.

His head started to turn her way, and Flossie moved into action, scuttling farther around the dome. Out of sight once more, she paused, her brow creasing. It didn't make sense. What was a Nazi officer of the twilight doing at St. Paul's?

As another shell exploded near the last one, Flossie popped her head around the corner again.

Thankfully, his attention was to the right. This time, she inspected him more closely. Maybe he was a Turnkey like her? After all, it was only Turnkeys who could come and go freely from cemeteries. While a

Turnkey could take one of their interred outside the cemetery gates with them to settle unfinished business and so on, it often wasn't advisable. It could be an unpleasant feeling for them to be separated from their body—whether it had been buried or cremated. The dead were meant to be at rest.

He wasn't a Turnkey. He didn't have an iron ring or a key of any sort in his hand. He was holding something, though—a strange object that he shifted now from underneath his right arm to his left, tucking it neatly and carefully into his left elbow.

Flossie was confused. If he wasn't a Turnkey, how had he gotten here? And what on earth *was* that thing he was holding? It was too bright to be of the twilight world, which it absolutely had to be. He couldn't carry an object that belonged in the living world. Whatever it was, it brightened with each shell that burst above, as if catching and holding the light. It was only as the man began to turn her way again that Flossie forced herself to slink back around the corner once more, disappearing from view at the last second.

None of this made any sense. A man of the twilight, carrying a strange object, without a Turnkey accompanying him, in a foreign land. Not to mention he was a Nazi officer in London. He was currently the enemy of her country. There were many reasons he shouldn't be here, dead *or* alive.

What should she do? Maybe nothing at all. There might have been a war raging in the land of the living, but her task was to see to the residents of Highgate Cemetery. Whatever he was doing here, it wasn't any of her business, was it? If his Turnkey had seen fit to let him leave his cemetery and go to London, it was nothing to do with her. Anyway, what harm could he do? He might have been the enemy if they had both been alive, but they weren't. Now that he was dead, the war was over for him, and that was that.

Still, something about it didn't seem right.

Flossie stepped out from behind the stonework just as another aircraft shell exploded to their left.

He saw her at once.

His eyes on her, he didn't move a muscle, that glassy-looking object glistening in the light of the shelling.

"What are you doing here?" Flossie shouted above all the noise.

He whirled into action, fleeing down the stairs.

"Stop!" Flossie cried. To run off like that, surely

he was up to no good. She was at the top of the spiral stairs in a second, but he was quite a way down them already. "Stop!"

He paused momentarily before starting down the stairs again. It was only then that Flossie remembered her advantage as a Turnkey. Closing her eyes, she reached the bottom of the stairs in a flash, just as he rounded the final bend of the spiral.

He stopped on the spot when he saw her, pushing the glass object behind him.

Oh, yes. Something was definitely up.

Flossie was now determined to find out what it was.

"Who are you? What are you doing here? What have you got there, behind your back?" she demanded.

It seemed she didn't have the advantage after all. Because, just like that, the man disappeared into thin air and was gone.

Chapter 3

In which Flossie returns home

Flossie simply couldn't work it out. Who was this man? What was he doing in London? And why had he run away like that?

Maybe if she described him, one of the newly interred at Ada's cemetery might know of him. He was obviously an officer of great importance. Perhaps he had been in the newspapers. Ada was the Turnkey of Tower Hamlets, one of the Magnificent Seven cemeteries currently receiving many dead. It was situated in the East End—one of the hardest hit areas of London, due to its proximity to the docks.

Before she went to visit Ada, however, Flossie reminded herself that she needed to make a brief stop at her old family home in Mayfair.

* * *

Flossie was relieved to see that her home's stone facade was untouched. Every time she visited, she was almost sure she would find that something awful had happened. Just last week, she had seen a similar townhouse, only streets away, sliced strangely in two, a piano hanging precariously from the drawing room. It was like a macabre life-size dollhouse, just waiting for a gigantic hand to descend from the sky and rearrange the pieces inside, ready for the absent family to return and for play to continue.

The all clear hadn't sounded yet, which meant that the streets were still devoid of life. There were no streetlights to illuminate the scene, of course — the strictly enforced blackout made sure of that — but the moon was bright, and Flossie took the opportunity to look around the silent street. Her family and the families close by them had been lucky so far. Green Street had suffered only minimal damage. Well, perhaps they had not been so "lucky" after all. All that was left of Flossie's immediate family was her mother.

Flossie had visited every so often until a few

months ago, when her mother had closed up the townhouse and moved to her parents' home in Buckinghamshire, away from the troubled skies of London.

At first her mother hadn't wanted to leave the city, thinking that her late husband, Flossie's father, wouldn't have been happy about such a move — not when the king himself remained at Buckingham Palace. Flossie's father had been a rear admiral in the Royal Navy and had gone down with his ship in 1916, in the Battle of Jutland, against the Imperial German Navy, when Flossie was just four years old. But when it came to moving away, Flossie felt that her mother had made the right decision. She was needed far more in the country, where the family home was being used to convalesce injured soldiers. Flossie remembered the German officer then. She had to hurry.

Closing her eyes again, Flossie appeared outside her old bedroom.

Her bedroom was usually a place Flossie avoided. Inside it, nothing had changed since her death all those years ago. Her hairbrushes lay neatly on the dressing table. A book or two, the pages marked for future reference, were strewn here and there—on her side table, on the window seat—as if she were still alive and could walk through the door at any time and resume her reading.

Flossie leaned back against the closed door before forcing herself to move into the room. As she passed by the looking glass above the decorative fireplace, she went to glance at herself as she always used to do. Another reason not to enter—her lack of reflection always disturbed her.

Flossie ran over to her writing desk with its little shelves set above. She focused on the item she wanted and prepared herself for the strange feeling that was about to come. Turnkeys could make copies of objects, dragging a likeness into the twilight world. It was an unpleasant sensation, which meant that it wasn't done often. Wrinkling her nose, she grabbed the doll and, with a *whoosh*, drew a copy of its form into the twilight.

A wave of sadness washed over her. The doll had been a present from Paris, where her sister, Emmeline, had been on her honeymoon. "I know you're far too old for dolls," she had told Flossie. "But I was walking past this toy shop and there was just something about her. I simply had to go in and buy her!"

Flossie hugged the doll to her, missing her sister more than ever. Emmeline had died giving birth to Flossie's niece, Clara. They were both buried in Highgate, and while Flossie loved having them nearby, it hurt not to be able to see them. She would never awaken them, though. A good Turnkey would never awaken one of their interred from rest unless absolutely necessary.

Flossie held the twilight doll, with its muted tones, up before her face.

"Right, then," she said to it, "time to go and see Ada about this wayward officer."

Chapter 4

In which Flossie visits Tower Hamlets

Flossie was heartened to see that at least the solid, unadorned gates of Bow Cemetery (as the locals called it) remained in one piece. The East End and the Docklands had been bombed almost beyond recognition in some places. Families here didn't have the same sort of options as her mother did. There were no ancestral homes in the country for them to retreat to. While they might send their children away to the country, or even as far as Australia or Canada, the adults of the East End had no alternative but to stay in London and see the war out.

The staccato sound of an ack-ack gun started a few streets away. The doll tucked under her arm,

Flossie watched the searchlights roam the sky, checking for enemy planes. She was just about to tap upon the gates with her iron ring to alert Ada, the Turnkey of Tower Hamlets, to her presence when the piercing, screaming whistle of a bomb sounded from far above. Then came the mighty bang and the shaking as the bomb hit, maybe five or six streets away. There was a long silence, and just as she thought it was all over, she heard the drone of a plane before the ack-ack guns went off again, faster this time and more insistent. The aircraft flew so low that she felt she could have almost reached up and touched it as it rained bullets down upon the street.

Flossie stood, unafraid, and watched the plane pass over her. Sometimes she wondered if this war would ever end.

"Oh, thank goodness you're here," a voice gushed from behind the gates.

Ada was busy with the lock. Ada had died of cholera, along with her entire family, almost one hundred years ago and was the first and only Turnkey of Tower Hamlets Cemetery. When Flossie had first met Ada, she had seen a small, wiry girl who distrusted everyone and wore a hard, cross sort of expression and a dress that was slightly too large for her slender frame. Now she only saw her best friend.

As Flossie passed through the iron gates, Ada's words came quickly. "It's so good that you've come. I'll need the extra hands."

"Have any of the other Turnkeys come to help?" Apart from Ada and Flossie, there were the elderly sisters Alice and Matilda at West Norwood Cemetery, the strange printer at Nunhead Cemetery, the sensible optician at Brompton Cemetery, the nervy Methodist minister at Abney Park Cemetery, and the imposing Victorian architect Hugo Howsham at Kensal Green Cemetery.

"Of course not," Ada replied.

"You've been hit badly?"

"The northwest corner. Not too badly—mostly shrapnel damage—but it will mean some of the nearby interred waking from rest. And you know how long it can take to settle some of them again."

As Ada locked the gates behind them, Flossie steeled herself for what she was about to see—Ada's Advisor. Each cemetery had both a Turnkey and an Advisor. The Turnkey's job was solely to care for the interred—to keep them happily at rest. The Advisor was the soul of the cemetery itself and could advise the Turnkey on anything involving the cemetery that he or she might need to know. Every new Turnkey was given the opportunity to choose the form their Advisor would appear in. Flossie's choice had been to bring forth her Advisor in the form of a fox she had known in life.

Knowing she couldn't put it off any longer, Flossie's eyes moved upward. And there she was— Ada's fearsome, imposing stone angel.

She wore a Grecian dress and long cape and she towered behind Ada, wings outstretched to finely carved tips. Her hands were calmly folded, a solemn expression on her face as she peered down at Flossie with her cold gray stone eyes.

"I hope that's not a present for me," Ada said drily. "Because I gave up dolls a century or so ago."

Flossie laughed, imagining serious, often-grumpy Ada dressing up a doll.

"It's for one of my interred," Flossie said.

"Well, that's a relief. I was worried you'd be wanting to play tea parties next." Ada's eyes darted around restlessly, as if she weren't quite sure what to do next.

Flossie placed her iron-ringed hand on Ada's arm. "Let's head on over to the northwest corner to see what's going on. And I promise, no tea parties."

Thankfully, the bomb damage wasn't as bad as Flossie had expected. A brick wall had collapsed, and several of the taller obelisks in the vicinity had toppled, but that was all. The shrapnel damage from the plane, however, was much more severe. Many headstones had been badly peppered, arousing a few confused interred from rest. Several of them were easily convinced to return to eternal slumber straightaway, but a mother and daughter from one of the cemetery's many mass graves had been awakened. They clutched at each other, and it took some time for both Ada and Flossie to coerce them back to rest.

"Part of me still thinks it's wrong—to persuade them to return to their dreams. It's as if I'm tearing them apart once more," Flossie said with a sigh when she and Ada were finished. She placed the doll on the ground and sat upon the edge of a monument, smoothing out the flared skirt of her dress and adjusting her navy-and-white dotted necktie. In life,

Mama had hated this outfit, saying it made Flossie look like a flapper. But she had dressed Flossie in it after her death, knowing how much she had adored it. That was love. The real sort. Flossie had learned a lot about love in death. About how it could cross all sorts of boundaries—time and distance, the twilight and living worlds.

Ada sat beside her in the dim light, her ever-present angel blending into the background of the cemetery behind them. "You know very well that's not true. There's nothing for them here. To be at rest . . ."

"Yes, I know." Flossie was taken back once again to that picnic on the grassy hill. She had been so happy. And then the cemetery had called upon her and she had been given her key from the Turnkey before her—a curious little Victorian man who had said he was tired and wanted to return to rest. "Say the words!" he'd told her, anxious to leave, and somehow she had known exactly the words that needed to be said.

I am the Turnkey of Highgate Cemetery; the dead remain at rest within.

She'd uttered the words almost without thinking. Within the blink of an eye, he was gone and she was

Turnkey. For who knew how long? Until she was tired, too, she supposed.

Flossie was dragged back to the present as she remembered the other reason she had come this evening.

"I have to tell you something. I saw something strange tonight—a man of the twilight, atop St. Paul's."

"A Turnkey from somewhere else?" Ada swiveled around to face Flossie.

"No, that's the thing. He wasn't a Turnkey. And he wasn't with one, either. At least I didn't see a Turnkey anywhere near him."

Ada thought about this for a moment. "And he wasn't distressed at being away from his body?"

"He didn't seem to be. It gets even stranger. He wasn't a Turnkey, but he could travel. I saw him do it right in front of me. One second he was there; the next he was gone."

"That doesn't make any sense."

"Wait. Here's the truly strange bit. He's not even from here. He was German. An officer of some sort. An important one in the SS. I could tell by his uniform."

Ada didn't understand as much about the ins and outs of this war as Flossie did. She found the new world outside her cemetery gates a confusing place and didn't like to leave her cemetery very often. Because of this, she relied on Flossie for a lot of information. But even Ada knew who the SS were.

"A Nazi! In London? Why? What's he doing here? Surely he's buried in Germany somewhere."

"I know! It doesn't make any sense at all."

"And he could really travel? Just like us? Without being a Turnkey?"

"He didn't have a key of any sort, but he was carrying something in his hands — a sort of glass object. I couldn't quite make out what it was. It didn't seem like it belonged in the twilight. It was too bright."

"That is odd. What do you think he's doing here?"

"I don't know. But I don't like it. I confronted him and he ran. He didn't want to be seen — that's for sure." Flossie couldn't get the picture of the man fleeing out of her head.

Ada's key rattled on its iron ring. They both looked down at it.

"Someone's at the gate," Ada said.

"Come on, then." Flossie picked up the doll, rose, and offered Ada her keyed hand to get up. "We'd best go see who it is."

As it turned out, however, it wasn't someone, but quite a number of someones at the gates of Tower Hamlets.

Chapter 5

In which help comes to Tower Hamlets

I'm afraid I couldn't stop them." The Turnkey of Brompton Cemetery — a tall, thin man with small, round glasses — stood close to the gate's railings, blocking out the view of the sea of men behind him. He had been Turnkey at Brompton for several years now, and Flossie quite liked him. He mostly kept to himself, but he saw to his interred and cared for them well. There was never a long queue outside his Turnkey's cottage. His gaze flitted nervously from Ada to Flossie and back again.

"It's all right," Ada told him. "What's happened? Why aren't they all at rest?"

"They've been waking with almost every bombing recently, anxious to help out. I've been able to settle them until now. This time they awakened as one when the bombing got particularly fierce, asked where help was needed, and then insisted that I bring them here directly. I've never seen a group of interred so determined. They don't seem to mind being separated from their bodies at all." He leaned in farther, the moonlight glinting off his glasses. "In fact, I think . . . I think they're rather enjoying themselves."

Ada snorted at this, and Flossie tried very hard not to laugh.

The Turnkey of Brompton moved to one side, and Ada and Flossie were greeted with the sight of at least a hundred men, all dressed in the same smart uniform. Each of them wore a long scarlet coat, and the combined effect was startlingly bright, despite the twilight giving the color a muted hue. Upon their heads, they all sported special black tricorn hats—triangular hats with three sides, which were decorated with gold braid.

Of all the people Flossie had expected to see at the gates, it wasn't a large gathering of aged Chelsea Pensioners. Because that was what these men were—

former members of the British Army who had, before death, lived at the Royal Hospital Chelsea, a famous retirement home for British soldiers. In their red coats, they were very distinctive; everyone in London knew who they were. In life, Flossie's mother had taken her each year to the Ceremony of the Christmas Cheeses, where cheese makers presented the Chelsea Pensioners with cheese to thank them for their service. The ceremony had been started back in the late 1600s, but these men seemed to be from this century. Flossie took heart in the fact that several of them were gaping at Ada's Advisor. It was good to know that grown men were just as afraid of the stone angel as she was.

One of the Chelsea Pensioners stepped up to the gate.

"Good evening, ladies." The man bobbed his head at the two girls and Ada's Advisor, then took off his hat, his silvery hair appearing from underneath. He gestured toward the men behind him. "We're here to help. We heard it's bad here in the East End. Worse than anywhere. Now, what can we do?"

Both Flossie and Ada were at a loss for words.

Ada found her voice. "I suppose I *will* need help

before long. After all, I'm sure the bombing won't end anytime soon."

This sent a buzz through the crowd of men.

Her eyes skating over the large group, Flossie had an idea. She edged closer to Ada. "Follow me," she said.

Outside the gates, Flossie approached the spokesman for the group. In life, these men would surely have had a keen interest in the war. Perhaps some of them weren't long dead. Just as she was about to speak, she remembered the doll under her arm and hurriedly put it behind her back, hoping they didn't think it was something she carried all the time.

"Does anyone know much about the SS?" she asked, her eyes moving over the group. Almost immediately, a louder murmur rippled through the men, and it wasn't long before one particular man was propelled to the front of the crowd.

"Go on, William," one of the men behind him said, nudging the tall, distinguished man with a tidy snow-white beard farther forward. "You'd know the most by far. He's recently dead, miss. Read all the papers in life."

"Well, I wouldn't call myself an expert, though I did read the newspapers every day when I was alive," William said modestly. "Do you have a particular question, miss?"

Fumbling with her iron-ringed hand, Flossie reached into her pocket and brought out a small notebook and pencil. These were also items she had pulled into the twilight world from the living one. She sketched a picture of the man she had seen atop St. Paul's, then passed the notebook to William.

"It's not a very good drawing, but do you know what sort of an SS officer would wear an outfit like this?"

A look of concern crossed his face. "You're right. He's SS. And with all his bits and bobs, he's definitely a faithful and longstanding member of the Reich."

Flossie had guessed as much. "And do you have any idea why someone like him might be carrying a round glass object of some type?"

William frowned. "A glass object? No, miss. No idea."

"Maybe it's a crystal ball!" one of the men from behind piped up. "Though we all know the Germans don't need one. We can tell them they're going to lose this war. No crystal ball needed!"

Laughter rang out at this, but not from William, who kept his eyes trained on Flossie, waiting for more information.

Flossie didn't laugh, either. "Where do you think a man like him would be buried? I'm guessing in Berlin."

William didn't seem certain. Another man spoke up now. "The Invalids' Cemetery for sure, miss. It's in Berlin. All the top brass is buried there. Always has been."

"I think we should use the men," Flossie said to Ada. "Post them around the city. See if we can spot this German officer again."

"Won't it be like finding a needle in a haystack?" Ada asked. "London isn't the smallest of places."

Flossie considered this. "Yes, but there are lots of places we won't have to look. He's not here on vacation and won't be taking tea at the Savoy. I don't know, maybe I'm wrong, but there was something about him. I want to find out what he's up to."

* * *

It took some time to discuss what to do. In the end, the three Turnkeys decided to divide the men into several large groups and station them at significant locations around London. The Turnkey of Brompton would deliver them to their stations and continue to nip between the groups in order to keep his charges at peace while they were away from their cemetery.

The men marched off behind their Turnkey with vigor.

"Do you really think they'll see him?" Ada asked.

Flossie readjusted the doll under her arm. "I honestly don't know."

"And what do you think they'll do if they find him?" A bemused expression crossed Ada's face.

Just then, the all clear sounded.

"I'm not sure." Flossie raised her voice over the noise. "But if they do, I bet they'll come up with something. Do you think you can hold the fort here while I duck over to Berlin to see if I can find anything out at this cemetery? I promise I'll come straight back to help you with any more of your interred."

Ada snorted. "Only if you bring me back a fancy present. I've never been outside of London, you know."

"Black Forest cake?"

Ada narrowed her eyes and then both girls laughed. They often joked about all the lovely things they'd eat if only they were able to.

"I'll bring back two large slices," Flossie said with a wink. And then she disappeared.

Chapter 6

In which Flossie decides to travel afar

Using her ornate key, Flossie unlocked the gates to Highgate Cemetery and then locked them again behind her. When she was done, she surveyed the ever-decaying gloomy landscape. Here and there lay monuments weathered by time. Some had fallen to the ground, others had sunk within it, and still others crumbled or tilted, the ivy claiming more of the cemetery each day.

She felt one of her interred awaken from rest. When she realized who it was, she groaned.

Millicent Gough, died 1872, age seventy-one, cause of death: twisted bowel.

"Hello, Mrs. Gough," she said to the woman striding toward her in the moonlight. The woman wore a long white burial shroud—rather like a loose nightgown. Her gray hair was pulled tightly back in a bun.

Flossie pushed the doll behind her again and hoped that Mrs. Gough wouldn't ask too many questions. She needn't have worried. Mrs. Gough was intent on what she had to say.

"I really must insist! The ivy! The tree roots! My husband paid good money for my plot!" Mrs. Gough's shroud shook with her agitation, though Flossie noticed that not one gray hair dared escape that bun.

Standing in the middle of the gravel path, surrounded on both sides by towering time-stained obelisks and eternally weeping angels, Flossie tried not to sigh. Mrs. Gough had been a wealthy woman who was far too used to getting what she wanted in life. She was determined that nothing should change in death.

"I'm sorry, Mrs. Gough, but it's as I've told you so many times before. We're at war. The living are busy just keeping alive themselves, let alone tending to our graves."

"I think it's a shocking disgrace. To treat the dead with such disrespect," Mrs. Gough huffed.

"No one means any disrespect, Mrs. Gough. It's simply a matter of necessity."

"That is exactly what you always say."

"I know—"

"Hmph!" Mrs. Gough cut Flossie off.

Flossie was about to offer to take Mrs. Gough back to her grave, but Mrs. Gough had disappeared. A wave of peace filled Flossie from head to foot, and she knew that Mrs. Gough had returned to rest. (It was always a lovely feeling—particularly lovely when that person was Mrs. Gough.)

With Mrs. Gough gone, Flossie closed her eyes and appeared inside her Turnkey's cottage. She had a lot to do. She stirred Amelia from rest and then summoned her Advisor. "Hazel?" she said.

"Mistress Turnkey." Hazel materialized upon the tattered rug, her coat glossy and smooth, her bearing dignified. She was just like the cemetery in many ways, which made sense. After all, she *was* the cemetery come to life—Highgate in Flossie's chosen form. Her bright, knowing eyes met Flossie's, replicas of the original Hazel's in life.

The original Hazel had lived at the edge of Flossie's boarding school grounds. Hazel, the fox of the living world, had been wild, of course. Flossie had first seen her bright-yellow, inquisitive eyes peering out from behind a hazel tree.

The thing was, Flossie's rheumatic fever hadn't taken her abruptly. She had initially been very sick. So sick her family had thought there was no hope for her. Slowly, over months, she had recovered enough to return to school, albeit with a very weak heart. But it had been hard to keep up with her friends. So she had started spending more time on her own, taking long, slow walks and pausing for a rest under a specific hazel tree. That was where she had met the fox. Flossie brought the vixen treats, and over time the fox had become friendly—content even to sit at arm's length and listen to Flossie talk about all the things she could tell no one else.

Eventually she had given her a name. Hazel.

When Flossie had been instructed to choose a form for her Advisor, it had been the fox who came to mind. And here she stood. Except this fox in the twilight world was someone else entirely, who could talk back.

"Hello, Hazel," Flossie said. "Ah, here comes my visitor now." She gestured toward the cottage door, and Hazel opened it with a flick of her tail.

"Amelia!" Flossie said. "Come in."

Amelia's eyes lit up when she saw what Flossie held in her hand. She ran the last few steps into the cottage.

"I'm afraid a lot of time has passed by and it wouldn't be possible to find your dolls now, but this one was mine. My sister gave her to me. I was wondering if you might take care of her for me." Flossie held her out.

"She's very beautiful."

"Isn't she? She's from Paris. My sister saw her there and bought her for me. But I was a little old for her. It would be nice for her to be played with properly."

Amelia took the doll from Flossie cautiously. "I won't break her."

"Of course you won't."

Amelia stroked the doll's thick brown hair. "What's her name?"

"See! That's why she needs to be with you. She doesn't even have a name. What do you think we should call her?"

"Marguerite," Amelia said decisively. "She seems like a Marguerite."

"Marguerite. I like that. I bet that if you returned to rest, Marguerite would appear in your dreams."

"Do you think so?"

"I . . ." Flossie stopped. Because Amelia and Marguerite were gone. She felt her return to rest.

"Very nicely done, Mistress Turnkey."

Flossie laughed a short laugh. "Sometimes, Hazel, just sometimes, I think I can handle this Turnkey job." She frowned, remembering the evening's events. "But then I realize I barely know anything at all." She sank into one of the armchairs. "Now, I have to go out again. Before I do, I have a question or two for you."

Flossie sat back after explaining all that had happened that evening. "Have any thoughts?"

Hazel considered her question before replying. "I agree, Mistress Turnkey. It's not a good sign that the German officer ran away in the way that he did. It sounds as if he has something to hide."

"One of the Chelsea Pensioners mentioned that this officer's most likely buried in a cemetery called the Invalids' Cemetery, in Berlin," Flossie said, shuffling to the edge of her seat. "Do you think I'd be able to travel there? Am I able to travel beyond the limits of London?" She hadn't considered the possibility before. She had never needed to.

"Yes, Mistress Turnkey. It is possible for you to do this. As within London, you must simply close your eyes and think of where you want to go. One of the previous Turnkeys needed to make a visit to Paris once for some information, and it went very smoothly."

"I hope things will be the same for me." Flossie stood, ready to be on her way. She knew Hazel wouldn't be able to come with her. She wasn't able to leave the cemetery. Without her, the cemetery would be soulless — nothing more than a mess of stone and greenery.

"I will await your safe return, Mistress Turnkey, as always."

Chapter 7

*In which Flossie learns more
about the German officer*

Flossie opened her eyes to find herself standing in front of a plain, thick gray stone wall and some iron gates. There was no showy entrance. No grand facade. It was almost dawn, and the faintest glimmer of light was beginning to appear. Through the gates a long gravel walkway stretched out into the distance, with mostly low-set, well-spaced manicured graves on either side. Tall, orderly rows of trees towered above the monuments, stark in the bleakness of winter. This was a businesslike cemetery of order, unlike her own higgledy-piggledy one.

Not a soul—living or dead—was in sight. Not even a Turnkey. A strange feeling emanated from this cemetery. Flossie felt that the dead were, for the most part, peacefully at rest. But there was something else . . . an uneasy, unsettled feeling.

Flossie wondered what she should do next. Should she attract the Turnkey's attention? Before she could decide, a flicker of movement made her jump. There was a girl standing behind the fence now — a girl in a beautiful white dress, a bow at her neck, with two long blond braids hanging neatly down her back. She met Flossie's eyes with a timid expression.

"*Wie heißen Sie?*" she said. "*Was wollen Sie hier?*"

"I . . . I'm sorry. I don't speak German," Flossie said. Why she hadn't thought of this problem until now, she had no idea. She'd been so caught up in wondering about the German officer, she hadn't considered the logistics of her visit. Sometimes she wondered why she had been chosen to be a Turnkey at all.

The girl drew back. "You're English!"

Flossie couldn't believe her luck. "You speak English? How? Why?" She couldn't have learned it at school — the girl must have been only around eleven or twelve years of age, and by the cut of her fashionable dress, she couldn't have been in the twilight for very long.

The girl's eyes darted back and forth as if she were waiting for something, or someone, to appear. "Yes. My father was a Rhodes scholar. He taught me English." A different expression fell upon her face then—a longing sadness.

"You miss him," Flossie said.

"My father was a good man. A kind man."

Flossie watched, sure that if the girl's eyes could have filled to the brim with tears, they would have. She thought of her own father. Most likely they had both lost a father to war, even if they had fought on different sides.

"Perhaps if you returned to rest?" Flossie suggested. The girl was obviously upset. Why wasn't her Turnkey seeing to her? Suggesting this?

"It's impossible."

Flossie frowned. Impossible? Of course it was possible.

"I shouldn't be talking to you." The girl's words tumbled out. "We're at war."

"I'm not at war with you," Flossie said simply. "Are you at war with me?"

"No. But . . ."

"What's your name?" Flossie asked, realizing she

hadn't introduced herself. "I'm Flossie Birdwhistle. I'm the Turnkey of Highgate Cemetery in London."

The girl shook her head. She wouldn't be revealing her name to Flossie. Not today, anyway.

With a shrug, Flossie decided to get to the point. "This war isn't about us or for us. The dead should be at rest. But it *is* why I'm here. I'm searching for a man. A Nazi officer with a sword at his side. SS, I think. I saw him in London, and I'm trying to find out more about him. I was told he might be buried here."

As Flossie spoke, the girl stepped away from the gate and her expression changed again—this time to fear. It was immediately obvious that she'd seen a man like that.

"You know who I'm talking about!" Flossie said. No answer came.

"You do." Flossie could see it. "You know him." She drew in closer, though she was careful not to touch the gate itself, lest she draw the attention of the Turnkey, who might send the girl away. "Who is he?"

The girl's eyes widened farther.

"What's the matter?" Flossie said, sensing that something was very wrong indeed.

A long silence followed. It felt as if the girl were teetering on the brink of telling her something.

"I . . . I can't say," the girl said.

"You can," Flossie replied. "Maybe I can help you."

It was the offer of help that pushed the girl over the edge.

"Have you come to stop him?" she said in a whisper. "Please tell me you have come to stop him." She put her hands to her head, as if recalling something painful. "He is planning terrible things. Awful things."

Flossie was shocked at both the girl's words and at how disturbed she seemed. She wasn't sure what to say. "What's he planning? What do you mean? Who is he? What's his name?" There were too many questions, but she couldn't seem to stop them exiting her mouth.

The girl inched away, her face now filled with absolute terror. "I should never have said that. Any of that. You're English. How can I trust you? As you said yourself, the war isn't for us. The dead should be at rest. I should be at rest."

"Wait! Please, don't go!" Flossie called out. "Tell me more! Who he is. What he's doing. If he's to be stopped——"

The girl, who had taken a step and looked as if she was about to run, suddenly stilled, her skirt swinging around her legs.

"Tell me something about him," Flossie pleaded. "Anything. And I'll see what I can do."

There was a moment's hesitation, and then the girl ran toward the fence and came as close to Flossie as possible. She gripped the railings tightly between her hands.

"He is part of the *Ahnenerbe*," she whispered, her eyes unblinking. "And he is coming back now. I can feel it. You must go. Right now! Please, go! *Schnell! Lauf los!*"

Chapter 8

In which Flossie meets Grace

Within seconds of the girl's disappearance, Flossie had left the Invalids' Cemetery. She retreated to Tower Hamlets, where her hand jutted out to rattle its gates, her key clanging against the iron railings.

"Flossie!" Ada appeared, her Advisor looming behind her. "You're back!" She unlocked the gates and swung them open, admitting her friend.

"I'd say you seem pale, but . . ." said Ada.

Flossie gave her joke a weak smile.

"What did you find out?" Ada asked.

Flossie tried to gather her thoughts. The girl's obvious fear had taken her aback, and there was also something strange about her—something dark that Flossie couldn't put her finger on. Why wasn't she at rest? Why was there no Turnkey in sight? Did the German officer have some part in all of that?

"I didn't find out much, I'm afraid. He's buried there, that much I'm certain of. Apparently he's part of something called the *Ahnenerbe,* though I have no idea what that is. I thought perhaps the Chelsea Pensioners might know about it."

"Ah," Ada said. "One of them's remained here in the hope that you might return with news. The others are all out keeping their eyes peeled for your officer. Here, I'll call him over to us."

In the blink of an eye, a Chelsea Pensioner appeared before them. It was William, the one who read all the newspapers.

He removed his tricorn hat, stroking his white beard with his free hand. "So, you've returned with news, miss. I was hoping you might. Our Turnkey's been checking in with all the men, and there've been no more sightings of your man so far, I'm pleased to say."

Flossie told both William and Ada what had happened in Berlin. "The girl I met didn't want to say much. She wouldn't tell me her name, and she was awfully frightened. She told me that this officer is part of something called the *Ahnenerbe*. Have you heard of it?" she asked William.

"No. Can't say I have. Never heard that word before in my life, miss."

Flossie had been about to reply to William when someone's touch surprised her. It was never a pleasant feeling to have a living person brush against you or sit upon you, not knowing you were there. But this was different. Flossie whirled around to see a girl of her own age reaching out toward her, a puzzled look upon her face.

"Ah, there you are. I wondered where you'd gone," Ada said. "I forgot to mention, Flossie, that we have a visitor. I saw her walking beyond the cemetery gates and got her to come in. She can't speak. I don't even know her name."

Flossie struggled to comprehend what she saw before her. The girl seemed to be neither dead nor alive. Instead, she hovered somewhere between the living and twilight worlds, a faded, transparent version of what she had once been. She wore a plain dress in a checkered brown fabric that was dusty and worn, a cardboard gas-mask box across her chest and resting on her hip.

"She's lost," Ada said simply. "In all senses of the word. I was about to try to take her outside to learn more. Perhaps take her home."

"I could do that, if you like," Flossie replied, knowing that Ada didn't like to go outside the cemetery walls. Certainly something needed to be done. And fast. However, while she wanted to help, she also needed to find out more about this officer parading around the streets of their city.

William must have understood her worry, because he spoke up immediately.

"You see to the lass, miss. I'll do the rounds and ask the men about this *Ahnenerbe* business." He popped his hat back upon his head. "Someone's sure to know something."

The girl was transfixed by Ada's Advisor. Surprisingly though, she didn't seem all that frightened. But if she lived in the East End, she had probably seen far worse things recently.

"Do you think you could show me where you

live?" Flossie asked her, making sure to keep her words in the present tense. This girl might be close to death; however, she wasn't there yet.

The girl bobbed her head.

"And could you tell me your name?" Flossie asked. Hopefully she would have better luck with this girl than the one at the Invalids' Cemetery.

The girl opened her mouth, but nothing came out. Flossie sighed. She had seen this type of thing after the last war, when she was alive. Friends' older brothers or fathers who had returned and had not been able to speak or had stuttered. She wondered if the girl might be suffering from something called shell shock.

Now Flossie readied herself for the strange feeling of contact with the living and put her hand on the girl's shoulder. Flossie pulled out her notebook and pencil from the pocket of her dress.

"Write your name down for me?"

The girl took the notebook and pencil from Flossie.

Grace

She wrote the word in a slightly trembly hand.

"Can you show me where you live, Grace?" Flossie asked.

Grace nodded.

"Your family?"

Mother
Sister

The words were written shakily.

Grace's eyes remained fixed on Flossie.

"We can go and look for them if you like," Flossie told her. "Write down your address while I speak to Ada for a bit." She took Ada's arm and the pair walked a few steps away.

"Why is she like this?" Flossie whispered hurriedly, their heads together. "Not the no talking; I mean why is she neither here nor there?"

Ada's eyes met hers. "I've only seen it twice before, and both times it's been about the person making a decision. It's not like when you and I died. Most people, there's no choice—the body can't go on. But Grace could go either way. It's up to her."

Flossie saw that Grace had finished writing. She took the notebook from her. It read:

Harford St. Stepney

"Come on, I'll unlock the gates for you all," Ada said. "And I'll make sure any news gets to you, Flossie."

With William striding ahead, Flossie took Grace's faded hand in her own and started their journey toward the East End in the brightening sky.

Chapter 9

In which Flossie takes Grace home

At the end of Harford Street — or what was left of it — the brickwork was fractured on either side of the road, wooden planks sticking out at angles, beds hanging from bedrooms, half chimneys gaping and hollow.

Throughout the ruins, bells rang, voices yelled, and dust swirled. The sky was alight. The fire brigade was fighting a still-raging fire somewhere down the road. Ambulance crews ferried the injured to the hospital; Civil Defence workers sifted through the rubble for bodies, alive and dead; a parson ran to and fro. Everyone was in a frenzy to have everything sorted before the next raid began.

In the midst of it all, the girls held hands tightly. Until, that is, Grace darted away. She stood in front of a space that had once been a house and was now a gaping void. Without warning, her legs buckled, and Flossie lunged to grab her elbow, stopping her from falling at the last second.

"Was that your house, Grace?" Flossie sat her gently down upon the road and crouched beside her.

After some time, Grace nodded.

"Were you in an Anderson shelter when the bomb hit?" Flossie knew that many of the families in this street would have Anderson shelters in their tiny back gardens, courtesy of the government. Strong corrugated iron structures with an arched roof, they were dug into the ground and then the disturbed soil was piled on top. They were extremely sturdy but could not survive a direct hit.

Grace gave no answer, though she gestured to Flossie's pocket. Flossie reached inside and pulled out the notebook and pencil.

"You keep it," she told Grace as she handed it to her again. "So, were you in the shelter?" she asked, her voice quieter this time. She didn't want to push, but she needed to find out what was going on.

Mother

Grace wrote. Flossie could see that writing the single word was a painful exercise in itself.

"Your mother was in the shelter?"

Grace's eyes, fearful, met Flossie's.

"And your father?"

In Egypt

Flossie bit her lip. If her heart could have clenched, it would have. Grace's father was fighting in Egypt, and her mother was most likely gone. Flossie opened her mouth to say something about her own father having been in the navy, then closed it again. That was a story that didn't end well. She remembered something else. "And your sister?"

Grace's fingers trembled as she wrote.

She forgot her glasses. We went to fetch them.

A group of men started down the road, approaching them. Flossie stood and offered Grace her hand.

Flossie saw that the group was a mix of Civil Defence workers, a civilian, and a man whose helmet read PDSA — the People's Dispensary for Sick Animals, or animal rescue. Beside him trotted a sweet little wirehaired fox terrier. They all stopped when they came to what was left of Grace's house. Flossie noted that Grace's expression perked up when she saw the civilian — a young man.

"You know him?" Flossie asked her.

Grace scribbled away.

Yes

"Definitely this one, you say?" one of the Civil Defence workers asked the young man.

"Yes. Two girls. Not just the one," he said. "Grace, her name is."

One of the Civil Defence workers spoke to the man from the PDSA. "We pulled one girl of around fourteen or so from the rubble — think her name was Ruth. But why weren't they in the shelter? That's where we found their mother, God rest her soul."

Flossie squeezed Grace's hand as the confirmation

that Grace's mother was gone hit her like a second blast. And was it her imagination, or did Grace fade away even further? Flossie willed her new friend to hold on, all the while thinking how unfair this war was. Homes weren't safe, backyard shelters weren't safe, even the Underground shelters weren't safe. Only weeks ago, a water main had burst at the Balham tube station and killed almost seventy people. Nothing was safe or sure anymore. Every time Flossie thought about the situation and found herself becoming angry, she then remembered that it was the same for everyone caught up in the fighting — British, German, Italian, Polish, French. The list of countries went on and on. For every girl like Grace, there was a German Liesl, an Italian Carina, a Polish Zofia, a French Camille. And that made it worse. No one was right. There were only vast acres of wrong, spanning countries and continents. There was nothing to be angry about. Only things to be saddened by.

A short bark caught Flossie's attention, and she saw that the little dog had homed in on something in the rubble. He stood on a pile of wood, his ears and nose twitching with excitement. A few sniffs and he began scratching furiously at the rubble beneath him.

"Seems Jack here thinks you're right, young man," the PDSA man said as he picked his way through the debris.

The other men followed him, and soon bricks and bits of banister were being passed from one of them to the other as they searched for Grace.

It wasn't long before the PDSA man called out.

"Here, Jack's found something!"

The men began scrabbling faster, bricks flying here and there.

And then Flossie saw it. The arm. She grabbed Grace and faced her in the opposite direction, not wanting her to see her body this way.

"Is she . . . ?" the young man said.

Flossie held her nonexistent breath, her hand clenched tight around her iron ring and her arms keeping Grace in place.

There was a terribly long silence. Then the dog barked a different sort of bark. "That means she's alive!" someone called out. And that's when all the voices started up at the same time.

"Come on, let's get her out of there."

"Careful, now, we'd better move some more bricks."

"I'll fetch the ambulance."

"That's it. Watch her leg. She's got a nasty cut."

Flossie kept Grace faced away from the scene until the ambulance doors closed behind her body.

The young man followed the ambulance driver around to his door. "Where will they take her? I'd better tell her . . ." He paused here, obviously remembering her mother was gone. "Her aunt. She's got an aunt who lives nearby, I think. And a young cousin."

"We're taking them all over to Lambeth Hospital. The other hospitals are full up. It's where her sister went as well, in case anyone needs to know."

Chapter 10

*In which Flossie and Grace
search for Ruth*

In the corridors of Lambeth Hospital, Flossie and Grace tried to make sense of what was going on around them. Gurneys were pushed up against the walls as doctors and nurses raced among patients, assessing their injuries. Horrible groans rose from some as they were pressed and prodded. Worse still, some didn't groan at all and were covered with sheets.

Flossie had no idea what to say. What to do. How to help Grace. Just as she'd done at the Invalids' Cemetery, she wondered why she'd been entrusted with the role of Turnkey instead of being left at rest.

Flossie didn't spend long ruminating on this, however, because Grace left their place beside her gurney and bolted down to the end of the corridor, her gas-mask box bumping against her hip as she ran. Flossie spotted what she'd seen as she followed close behind her — a pair of glasses balanced precariously on top of a white sheet that a doctor had picked up and was now passing to a nurse. He read the paper tag that was attached to Ruth, dusty, pale, and unconscious on the gurney. "This one next. It could be her spleen."

Grace bent down close beside her sister's face, and as she stared at her unresponsive sibling, she again seemed to fade away just that little bit more.

"You've got to be strong for her," Flossie told Grace. "Someone needs to believe she'll be all right."

It wasn't long before a shout from the swinging doors farther up the corridor saw the nurse from before arrive back at Ruth's gurney. Grace gave her sister one last longing look before she was whisked away, taken to surgical theater.

Flossie needed to get moving. She had to find out more about the German officer. But just as the gurney disappeared from sight, something happened to Grace. Her face creased with pain and she doubled over. Flossie glanced back down the corridor once more to see that Grace's body in the living world was being assessed. Flossie helped Grace to her gurney to see what was going on.

"She's broken at least two ribs, and there could be some internal bleeding," a different doctor said to a nurse who wrote on Grace's cardboard tag. "I want her blood pressure checked again in the next half hour, but she can wait." He moved off, leaving the nurse to scribble some notes.

"This could take a while," Flossie told Grace. She couldn't drag Grace away from here—not while her sister was in surgery. But she also needed to return to Tower Hamlets somehow. She had to find out if William had discovered anything else about the German officer. As much as she didn't want to, she would have to leave Grace.

"Grace"—she reached out and touched her on the arm—"I need to go and check on something. Do you think you'll be all right until I return? I won't be long."

It took Grace some time to let Flossie know she had registered her words.

"Good. I'll be right back—I promise you."

A flicker of her eyelids and Flossie was at the gates of Tower Hamlets once again. Time had moved on and it was morning now, with people walking around the streets, checking on the damage, on loved ones, on friends. The East End was waking up.

"Ada!" Flossie rattled the gates, her key clattering against the iron railings.

Ada appeared at once, her angelic Advisor filling the sky behind her. Before Ada could speak, Flossie's words tumbled forth.

"Don't worry about letting me in—I don't have much time," she said. "I have Grace and her sister at Lambeth Hospital, but I wanted to check if you have any news for me."

"I do," Ada said. "Your German officer has been spotted again. This time in Whitehall."

Flossie bit her lip. In Whitehall, where all the country's important government departments and ministries were located! This time she didn't pause to think about what he might be up to. Now it was time to act. "I need to take someone back with me. To stay with Grace."

"It was the Turnkey of Brompton who brought

the news, along with a few other men. The men are still here, and so is William, though the Turnkey of Brompton had to leave in order to see to his other men. I'll bring the men to us."

William and three other of the Chelsea Pensioners appeared before them.

"I've got another mission for you, if you don't mind," Flossie said. "But I'll need someone else as well." She turned to the other three men. "Did any of you have daughters when you were alive? Grand-daughters?"

"I had three daughters, miss. And five grand-daughters!" a man with a fine silver mustache and unruly eyebrows said proudly.

"Well, I have a special task for you." Her eyes moved to the man questioningly as Ada opened the gates, ready for their departure. "William and . . ."

"Michael, miss. The name's Michael Woodman," he said as he was ushered outside along with William and Flossie.

"I'm hoping that you'll know just what to say to a small girl who's feeling very lost."

Ada locked the gates behind them, her expression

worried. "Be careful!" she warned Flossie. "I'll let the Turnkey of Brompton know where you are so he can stop by."

"Thanks! I'll be back to check in with you soon."

With a last wave in Ada's direction, Flossie took both William's and Michael's hands and closed her eyes.

"Grace?" she called out on opening them once more, back in the corridor at Lambeth Hospital. Flossie saw that Grace's gurney hadn't moved an inch, but twilight Grace was not in sight. Dropping the two men's hands, she took a few quick steps down the corridor. And if she could have breathed a sigh of relief, she would have. There was Grace, sitting on the floor, her back against the wall. "You scared me!" Flossie crouched down before her. "Do you think you could come and meet someone for me?

"This is Mr. Woodman, Grace." Flossie introduced her to the kindly Chelsea Pensioner.

"Michael, please," he interjected. "Mr. Woodman feels wrong in the afterlife, somehow."

Flossie knew exactly what he meant. Things were more informal in the afterlife for some reason.

There was more equality. Young and old, rich and poor—all were on the same footing in the twilight.

"Michael will stay with you, Grace," she continued. She filled Michael in on the fact that they were waiting for Ruth to return from surgery and that Grace was being monitored.

Grace's worried eyes moved to Flossie's as she spoke. "Don't you worry; I'll be back soon," Flossie told her when she was done. "Do you have your notebook and pencil?"

Grace held up the notebook.

Michael took the lead. "Come on, love. I'll tell you all about the time I met the king. He's a decent fellow, and he and Churchill are going to get us out of this mess, you know. . . ."

William offered Flossie his arm. Together they walked to the end of the corridor, where her face adopted a worried frown.

"Tell me exactly what's going on," she said.

Chapter 11

In which Flossie goes underground

William leaned against the wall as a nurse walked by. "The thing is, we've been following the top brass around. Top secret, it is, but the Cabinet War Rooms are beneath the Government Offices on Great George Street. That's where they control the whole war from, you know. The prime minister's there for most of the day."

Flossie covered her mouth with her keyed hand, shocked. "And that's where the German officer was seen?"

"Heading for the War Rooms, yes. Seemed like he knew where he was going, too."

"Which means he's known where they are for—"

"We don't know how long, miss, but longer than we have. Worse still, the men got a good look at him—at his uniform and his medals." He paused to whistle. "That one would have had the ear of Hitler, that's for sure."

It was as Flossie had feared but had been too scared even to give thought to. To put a name to. Because she wasn't sure how it could be possible. Or what it might truly mean.

The German officer was a spy.

"You just missed our Turnkey. The thing is, the men and I were talking to him. The German officer can't still get information to him, can he, miss? To Hitler, I mean. We asked our Turnkey, and he said no. We wanted to ask you as well."

"I don't think he'd be able to," Flossie said. But she was beginning to become very afraid that she might be wrong about that. What if he'd found a way? A way to bridge the gap between the living and twilight worlds. It wasn't supposed to be possible— every person in the twilight world knew that. There was no way for them to communicate with the living, and no way for the living to communicate with them. Flossie remembered something. "And the word that the girl mentioned? The *Ahnenerbe*?"

"One of the men, Leo, had a German grandmother so he speaks a bit of German, and he said the word means *a legacy*. You know, something inherited from the people who came before you."

Flossie considered this. "That doesn't make sense. The girl told me he was 'part of the *Ahnenerbe*.' As if it were some sort of a group."

"We'll keep asking around. Right now it might be best to return to the War Rooms. See what's going on there."

Flossie held out her keyed hand toward William. "You're right. Just tell me where to go."

William directed Flossie to take them to the corner of Horse Guards Road, Great George Street, and Birdcage Walk. When she opened her eyes, the first thing she saw was a large wall of sandbags directly in front of them.

"Get down!" Someone tugged on her dress, and

both she and William were unceremoniously pulled to the ground. They landed cross-legged, their backs against the sandbags.

"Sorry, miss," said a Chelsea Pensioner she hadn't met before, "we don't want him to see us. He was close by not long ago, lurking around Number Ten. We think the prime minister's on the move."

Flossie slumped against the sandbags. Things were only getting worse. Now the German officer was at the prime minister's official residence at 10 Downing Street!

Another Chelsea Pensioner flew around the corner of the long wall of sandbags and rushed over to them, his coat flapping. "The German officer's down there now. In the War Rooms. They're all there — Churchill and all. There'll be a meeting soon, I'd say. But there's more. That thing he's got? It's not a crystal ball. It's some kind of a skull."

"A skull?" William and Flossie said at the same time.

"Not only that, but he's talking to it. Arguing with it in German. The man's stark raving mad! Leo's down there listening in, translating what he can. And believe you me, you're not going to like what he's overheard."

Flossie and the men walked past the sandbags and barbed wire and down to the entrance to the bunker. Two Royal Marines stood at attention, guarding the open entrance—a wooden door. The men had helmets on their heads and rifles by their sides.

Taking the lead, Flossie slipped past the marines and through the open doorway. They proceeded until another Chelsea Pensioner came into sight. He had been peering into a different corridor, and now he beckoned them toward him, at the same time holding a finger to his lips, warning them to be quiet.

Obviously the German officer was close by.

The foursome continued along soundlessly. When they reached the other Chelsea Pensioner, the men shuffled Flossie forward so she was at the front of the group. William followed her.

Flossie took a peek herself. A long corridor presented itself. It was rather like a rabbit warren down here—doors leading off either side of the passageway. Some of the doors were open, and she could see that the rooms inside were tiny and almost cell-like. A woman in a plain blue dress, a knitted cardigan, and immaculate red lipstick passed by in a hurry.

One of the men tapped Flossie on the shoulder and pointed around the corner to the left.

"Down there," he whispered to William and Flossie. "He's in that room. Leo's in the opposite room across the hall, listening in."

"We'll go down there," William said.

Flossie followed him, gripping her key so it wouldn't clank on its iron ring and alert the German officer to her presence. Just as the Chelsea Pensioner had said, there was already a man in the small room — Leo.

William and Flossie crowded in beside him.

"What's going on?" William whispered.

"He seems to have quieted down," Leo said, his voice low. "But he was ranting and raving before, shouting at that skull of his. Strange thing, that. Doesn't seem like it belongs in our world, does it? What do you think he's doing with it? *That* doesn't come standard issue with —"

Everyone jumped as a voice shouted in German. Flossie listened in as the foreign words rose and fell. A pause. Then more words. Then another pause. It really *was* as if he were arguing with someone.

"What's he saying?" she asked Leo.

"Mostly the same thing," he said, concerned. "That he'll be back, that it will all be over soon, that his actions will mean a quick and easy end to the war. Before he went into that room there, he was in the map room. He read out a whole lot of coordinates. Almost like he was reading them *to* someone, or dictating them."

There was no doubting it now. He was gathering information. He truly was a spy.

"Can I go and see what he's doing?" she asked Leo.

"It should be all right. His back is to the door."

"Keep low," William warned her.

Getting on her hands and knees, Flossie crossed the corridor swiftly. She eased onto her stomach and peeked around the edge of the doorway.

The German officer sat in a tiny room with not much more than a desk, a wooden chair, a shiny black telephone, and a green glass banker's lamp. His uniformed back to her, he shifted in the chair, and Flossie flinched. Instead of turning, though, he leaned forward and began to speak. Flossie lifted her head to see what held his attention.

It was just as she'd been told. It *was* a glass skull he was speaking to. She hadn't been able to see its shape properly up on the top of St. Paul's, but she saw it now — the round, smooth top, the hollowed-out eyes, the narrowing of the jaw. He had his hand upon it as he talked, and every so often he leaned in farther, almost crooning to it. Her eyes locked onto it, mesmerized. She'd never seen anything so bright in the twilight world before.

Some movement down the corridor made Flossie draw her head back. Uniformed men of the living world were coming. She crossed back to the room with William and Leo, hiding herself away.

As the men passed by, Flossie caught snippets of their conversation. They were talking about a meeting.

"They mentioned that before. There's going to be a meeting very soon. In the Cabinet Room. With the prime minister," Leo said.

"Tell the young lady what you just told me," William said to Leo, his expression grave.

Leo's brow furrowed. "I'm sorry, miss, my

German's not that good. Before you got here, just after he'd been in the map room, he did mention something else."

"What?" Flossie's hand clenched tight around its iron ring. "What did he say?"

"I didn't catch all of it, but he'd been talking about an invasion. And then, a while after that, he said something about Highgate Cemetery. About Highgate and about Kensal Green, too."

Chapter 12

In which Flossie meets the prime minister

Before Flossie could ask any questions, Leo pushed both her and William back into the room.

"He's on the move," he said. "He's gone into the Cabinet Room."

"But wait. You really can't remember anything else that he said about the cemeteries?" All she could think about was what the German officer might have meant. Why would he be talking about Highgate and Kensal Green? What use could the cemeteries be to him? He couldn't enter them, because they were safely locked in the twilight. However, she was beginning to see there was a lot to this man that she didn't understand. He shouldn't be able to travel. And yet he could.

"I really am sorry, miss. As I said, my German's not that good."

This was frustrating, but Flossie knew she was lucky that one of the Chelsea Pensioners spoke any German at all.

"Come down this way so we're closer. When Churchill arrives, the meeting will start." Leo gestured for Flossie and William to follow him, and they entered a room where the walls were completely covered in maps. There was a huge wooden desk in the middle of the space and telephones of all colors perched on a raised platform in the middle of it — green, white, black, red. It wasn't this that caught her attention, though. Even from where she was standing, she could see the black-topped pins on the map on the far wall, gathered and ready to hurtle full speed at Britain across Europe and up from Africa.

The German army was coming.

"Ah, here's the prime minister now," Leo said, still standing by the door.

Flossie positioned herself to catch a glimpse of a squat, dark-suited man passing by the door.

Churchill.

"I'm going to go and see what the German officer's doing in there," she said decisively.

"I don't know, miss." William didn't seem certain. "Why don't you let one of us go instead?"

No. He'd mentioned her cemetery. The cemetery where all her interred were at rest. Including her sister and niece. She couldn't stop until she found out exactly what the officer was doing here and what his intentions were.

As she approached, the noise of the men in the room rose to an almost deafening level, bouncing off the windowless walls, everyone speaking at once.

She reached the open doorway of the Cabinet Room and pressed herself back against the cream-colored painted brickwork. And then, slowly, very slowly, she peeked inside. The group of men was arranged in a square-shaped formation of tables.

There was Mr. Churchill, at the center of the head table at the front of the room. He was seated in a large wooden chair in front of a vast map of the world. And at the table to his left, only four seats away, was the German officer.

Despite his high-necked uniform, he looked

comfortable in his chair, leaning back, the heel of one of his glossy boots crossed, his ankle resting on top of his leg. The skull was on his lap, and he had one hand protectively upon it.

Flossie's eyes widened as she pulled back. He had the nerve to actually sit at the table!

Flossie thought for a moment. There was something about that skull—the way he spoke to it, cradled it. How he'd hidden it from her when she'd confronted him and he'd run off.

She looked down the corridor at William and Leo and then, farther up the corridor again, at the other group of Chelsea Pensioners. As one, they beckoned her back to them.

Flossie shook her head. No. She had to find out more about that skull. What it was. Why it was so important to him.

She knew what she had to do.

If she could have taken a deep breath, she would have. Instead, she got down on her hands and knees. She clasped her key between two fingers so it wouldn't clink against its iron ring, and began to crawl.

Inside, Flossie was met with a view of a sea of legs. Underneath the tables, she could see the officer's one glossy boot upon the floor, and it was this that she kept her eyes trained on as she went down the right-hand side of the room. When she got to the end of the table on this side of the room, she rounded the corner and continued up the next side, still hidden from his view. At the end of this table, she peeked around the corner. He was in plain view. He'd spot her in an instant.

She pulled back and tried to think of another way. She didn't want to travel. Popping about here and there might remind the Chelsea Pensioners of their own Turnkey and how far away they were from their own cemetery. She didn't need any more problems right now.

Flossie checked underneath the tables again. There was that one boot, the other leg still up and crossed, resting upon the other.

And there was the skull upon his lap.

She gritted her teeth and passed straight through both the table legs and trousered legs closest to her. It was a horrible, sickening feeling, a pull and push of worlds colliding inside her body — twilight and living. It was over in an instant, and Flossie found herself in the middle of the vacant square space formed by the tables. She kept low until she was directly in front of that boot.

The shiny blackness of it was so close now that she could have reached out and touched it. She shuffled as close to it as possible.

The skull grinned back at her.

She would have to be quick. So quick.

There would only be one chance.

Flossie crouched into a starter's position, took a last long look at the skull — and lunged.

She tried to ignore the horrible tearing feeling of objects passing through her. She reached out her hands, her key flailing around on its ring, and grasped at the skull.

The officer jerked away instantly. However, her keyed hand managed to land fully upon the skull as they both stood up together.

If Flossie had thought passing through the table felt terrible, this was something else entirely. The second she touched the skull, she wanted to pull away, a flood of emotions washing over her body — both good and bad. No, not good and bad, but good and evil. It was as if dark and light, night and day, black and white, battled within the skull.

And evil was winning.

As well as this feeling, there were voices. Two distinct voices that swirled and whirled, ricocheting off each other. The older male voice spoke German; the other was higher and younger, though she couldn't quite tell if it was female or male. She also couldn't hear the words or the language of the second voice properly — it was as if it were being forcibly subdued. However, even though she couldn't understand the words of the second person, Flossie could tell the voices were having a heated argument.

As much as Flossie wanted to recoil, she forced her other hand forward and grappled with the officer. With the skull.

But he was stronger.

He pulled back in one swift movement, wrenching the skull from her grasp.

His eyes met hers, his stare one of hatred. Disgust.

"Birdwhistle," he said with a sneer.

And then, just like that, he was gone.

Chapter 13

In which Flossie calls a meeting

Flossie tapped upon the gates at Tower Hamlets with her iron ring, the group of Chelsea Pensioners silent and solemn behind her.

"I was hoping you'd be back soon. How did you fare?" Ada began to unlock the gates.

Ada's Advisor glared down at Flossie. It was almost as if she already knew Flossie had failed in her attempt to grab the skull and had expected as much all along.

When they were all inside, William placed a hand on her shoulder. "We'll leave you two to talk."

Ada looked at her questioningly as William and the other Chelsea Pensioners walked away, already deep in discussion. "I take it things didn't go as well as you'd hoped," she said.

"No." Flossie sighed, taking in the cold, hard ground, the spindly trees, the ivy-garlanded graves. She began to tell Ada exactly what had happened, from going down to the War Rooms to touching the skull to the German officer's disappearing trick. "I thought I might be able to grab the skull from him, I really did. It's not just that, though. There's more." Her expression was grim. "He mentioned Highgate and Kensal Green."

"What?" Ada said. "What did he say?"

Flossie explained that Leo hadn't caught all the details.

"But why do you think he'd be mentioning the cemeteries?" Ada was instantly worried.

"I really don't know. Worse still, he knew my name."

"*What?*"

Flossie shrugged. "All I can think is that he did some investigating of his own after our encounter on top of St. Paul's. The way he said it . . ." Flossie shuddered, remembering. "It was as if he hated me.

Truly hated me." She pushed the thought of it aside, trying to get back on track. "I think we really need to move fast now. It might be a good idea to gather the other Turnkeys for a meeting. Together we have a lot of people at our disposal—over a million. Surely one of our interred might know something about this man and the group he's involved with."

"Good idea. Should we meet outside Highgate? As soon as possible?"

"Yes. You find out where the Turnkey of Brompton is and get the Turnkey of Abney Park as well. I'll gather the others and—" Her words were cut off by the air-raid siren, which reminded Flossie of something else entirely. "Oh! Grace! How could I have forgotten?"

"Don't fret," Ada said. "The Turnkey of Brompton has been going back and forth and reporting in. Grace's sister, Ruth, is out of surgery, and they're both in a ward together."

Flossie beamed. "At last! Some good news! I'm so happy for them. And has she . . . ?" Flossie paused, not knowing how to word her question. "Has she rejoined with her body?"

"No, not yet. But Michael was hopeful that it might happen soon. He'll stay with her until then." Ada linked arms with Flossie and they started toward the cemetery gates. "And on that note, let's round everyone up, shall we?"

Some time later, outside Highgate, Flossie approached the Turnkey of Nunhead Cemetery and was reminded of Ada's comment about rounding everyone up.

Rounding up the Turnkey of Nunhead Cemetery wasn't going to be easy.

"I think we're about to start the —" Flossie began before he interrupted her.

"Ah, wait one moment." He began to flick through the notebook he always carried with him. "I'm sure it's here somewhere. No . . ." He kept flicking. "Ah, I knew it!" Pleased with himself, he closed the notebook. "I was in the middle of some very important work."

Flossie tried not to groan. A thin, nervous, twitchy little man, he was always rambling on about his "very important work."

"I was a printer in life, you know. I'm making a list of all the typefaces used in my cemetery."

"Yes, I *know*," Flossie said hurriedly, hoping he wouldn't make the speech he'd made so many times before.

But it was too late.

"Do you realize how many different styles there are in these cemeteries? I've documented less than a quarter of my cemetery so far, and yet here I have hundreds of styles noted already. See here! There's Egyptian Italic, Caslon Italian, Gothic with shading, Chamfered Egyptian, Egyptian with shading, Reverse Italic Egyptian, Reverse Italic Gothic."

"Please." Flossie took his arm. "This way." She practically dragged him over to the others and stood him beside the sisters from West Norwood. "We're just waiting on Ada. She's getting the Turnkeys of Brompton and Abney Park."

"Lovely, dear," Alice and Matilda, the joint Turnkeys of West Norwood Cemetery, said at the same time. Similar in appearance, they were both as white as their twilight existence allowed them to be — with matching white upswept hair and long white shrouds.

Between them, they clasped an iron ring with one key on it, each holding on to it with one hand. The sisters had apparently always done everything together. They married two brothers and lived next door to each other. When their husbands died, they lived together again. They had somehow even managed to die of natural causes within a day of each other.

Ada arrived then with the two Turnkeys, and Flossie went over to greet them. She'd just finished saying her hellos when a low, authoritative voice spoke from behind her.

"Good afternoon," it said.

Flossie whirled around to see a tall Victorian gentleman in an exquisitely cut pitch-black frock coat and top hat.

Hugo Howsham. The Turnkey of Kensal Green.

As he swept off his hat, dark curls appeared, tumbling over the tops of his ears. He held the key to his cemetery on its iron ring in one hand. In the other hand he held smart doeskin gloves and a walking stick with an ivory handle.

Hugo Howsham had been part of the reason Flossie and Ada had become friends. He'd put up with Ada's presence as a young Turnkey for the simple reason that Tower Hamlets was a modest cemetery and she'd been chosen first of all the Turnkeys — a great honor. But when Flossie was selected for probably the most well-known and prestigious of the seven cemeteries, he'd apparently been appalled that a "child" had been appointed to the task. He'd let all the other Turnkeys know it, too. His only redeeming feature was his lovely sister, Violet. Violet preferred to stay in an awakened state to keep her brother company, and Flossie had met her several times over the years.

Violet stepped out from behind her brother.

"Oh, Violet! It's so good to see you." Flossie's eyes met the beautiful Violet's. And she *was* beautiful. She wore a stunning teal silk dress with white lace trim, her wavy chestnut hair tied loosely to one side with a matching white ribbon. But it wasn't just this that was special about Violet. Her nature shone above and beyond these things.

In life, Violet had been a spiritualist — a person who believed that there was life after death and that the living and dead could communicate. She had told Flossie before that while she had always known in her heart that there was a world of the dead, it had always eluded her, remaining just out of her reach. She had never stopped trying to contact the twilight world, however, hoping that one day she might succeed. Unfortunately, she had been young and naive and had made friends with a famous spiritualist group that claimed to be in constant contact with the dead, except they were only fleecing people for money. When they had revealed their many tricks to Violet at a séance, she was so horrified that she had fled into the street and been run over by a horse and carriage. She had died far too young. Now Hugo Howsham kept a close eye on his sister in death, feeling that he had failed to protect her in life.

"Flossie!" Violet came over to take her hands.

Flossie's eyes flicked nervously toward Violet's brother.

"Miss Birdwhistle," he said, acknowledging her presence.

Flossie gathered the Turnkeys together so they were all in the one group.

"I'm sure you're wondering why I've called you all here today," Flossie said to the group. "I'll start from the beginning, because I'm not sure what you know. The other night I was atop St. Paul's . . ." She went on to explain how she had chased the German officer and he had disappeared, how she had visited the Invalids' Cemetery and met the girl, how the Chelsea Pensioners had helped her track down the German officer again, about the bright skull that he carried and what had happened when she'd tried to take it from him.

"As I said, he's not a Turnkey, but he's traveling somehow, and he's doing it without a Turnkey. He's been overheard reciting coordinates, talking about invasion, and he's even mentioned both Highgate and Kensal Green cemeteries, though we're not sure why."

There was an explosion of voices as everyone spoke at once.

"What do you mean he mentioned Kensal Green?" Hugo Howsham's expression was stern.

Her keyed hand raised, Flossie waited until the commotion died down.

So did someone else.

Violet stepped in front of her brother. "If I may? I have some information."

"Of course." Flossie remembered that not all

the Turnkeys would know of Violet's past. "In life, Violet was a spiritualist. She was convinced that our world existed before she actually died," she informed the group.

"I'm afraid to say it," Violet said, "but this skull that Flossie is talking about . . . I think I know what it is."

Chapter 14

In which Flossie learns the history of the skull

I believe the skull might be made of crystal. I've never seen one myself, but there was much talk of several being discovered while I was still alive. In fact, someone in the group I was involved in—"

"Violet!" Hugo Howsham snapped, cutting his sister off.

Violet only held up a hand. "Hugo, please. This is important. I think the skull could be Mayan."

Flossie's eyes widened. "What? An ancient artifact of some kind?"

"Yes. And from what I know about these skulls, and from what you've said . . . well, it's possible that the officer's soul may have been placed in it. There is a process I've heard whispers of where these skulls are concerned. The soul can be captured at death and held within the skull, so that it lives forever."

There was a collective gasp.

"How can he be carrying it with him in the twilight world?" Flossie continued. "It doesn't make sense."

"I don't know," Violet answered. "It might have something to do with his soul being held within it. Can you tell me more about what you felt when you touched it?"

"It was awful. A horrible feeling. An *evil* feeling." She remembered clearly the expression on the German officer's face — that piercing glare of hatred. How he had said her name. It matched the male voice inside the skull perfectly. "There was something else, too. It was almost as if there were an argument going on inside it."

"Wait. Do you mean two distinct voices?"

"Yes," Flossie said.

"They were arguing?" Violet asked.

"Definitely," Flossie said. "It was him, speaking in German, and someone else — a young person, though I couldn't tell if it was a boy or a girl. The younger voice was muted compared to the other voice. It might not have even been speaking German. I couldn't tell."

"Can you remember anything that either of the voices said? I had a German tutor for many years. My German's quite good."

"Sorry, no."

"Oh, dear. This isn't good at all. There could be another soul in there as well. Perhaps from Mayan times."

Flossie mulled over the situation. "And do you think it's the skull that's giving him the ability to travel?"

"I'm not sure. It's possible, I suppose. It's a very powerful object, and not much is known about these skulls. Anything is possible, really."

"What about being able to pass information to the living? Could he do that?"

It was the lack of Violet's immediate answer that made Flossie realize once and for all that this was the man's aim. He was here to spy, and he was either trying to find a way to pass that information to the living via the crystal skull, or he'd already found one.

The group was silent.

"I suppose what we need to do now is find out several things," Flossie said. "For a start, why was he talking about Kensal Green and Highgate? Can he already pass messages to the living? And something else—I was told he's part of a thing called the *Ahnenerbe*, which is apparently something to do with a legacy. We need to find out more about that, too. That's really why I wanted to gather you all here—to see if you could ask your interred about the word."

"And my Chelsea Pensioners?" The Turnkey of Brompton spoke up, adjusting his glasses.

"If it's all right with you and the men, I think it would be good to keep them posted throughout the city, keeping a watchful eye."

"Of course."

"So"—Flossie's attention moved back to the group—"when you all return to your cemeteries, could you ask your interred about the *Ahnenerbe*? You might even find some sort of connection to Highgate or Kensal Green. In the meantime, I'll continue to hunt down information as well."

One by one, the Turnkeys departed for their cemeteries until only Ada was left.

"When you brought up Violet's past, I thought Hugo Howsham might eat you alive," Ada said.

Flossie gave a weak laugh.

"I'll come in with you for a quick visit, then I'd best be getting back." Ada gestured toward the gates of Flossie's cemetery.

Grateful for the offer of some company, Flossie walked toward the smaller dusky set of gates for the dead, set apart from the solid black iron gates for the living. She opened them with her key, then locked them again once she and Ada had passed through. Then she closed her eyes and did something that she had never done before and hoped she would never need to do again—as gently as possible, she stirred all of her dead and asked them if they knew anything about the *Ahnenerbe.*

She received a slew of whispers in return, which curled and twirled around her, filling her mind. Some spoke of the word *legacy*—of inheritance—just as she'd been told previously, but no one could tell her anything more than this.

"Nothing?" Ada asked when Flossie opened her eyes once more.

"I'm afraid not," Flossie replied. "Come on, let's

go see Hazel." She walked the short distance over to her cottage, where there was, thankfully, no queue. She let Ada inside and closed the door swiftly behind them.

"Nobody waiting to see you. What a shame. I was so hoping to see Mrs. Gough today," Ada teased, sitting down in one of the armchairs. She'd met Mrs. Gough several times in the past.

Flossie shot her friend a withering look as she fell into the matching chair. "Hazel?" she called out.

Just as Hazel appeared on the threadbare rug, a knock came upon the door, which Hazel opened with a flick of her tail.

"Amelia! Come in!" Flossie said, already knowing who was on the other side.

Amelia entered the room hesitantly.

"Amelia, this is my friend Ada, the Turnkey of Tower Hamlets Cemetery," Flossie said. "Ada, this is Amelia, one of my interred."

"Ah, the doll again," Ada said, spotting it in Amelia's arms.

"Is everything all right?" Flossie asked, approaching her small friend. "Why aren't you at rest?"

"Well"—Amelia's voice sounded concerned—

"I don't know what you were asking about just before, but you seemed upset. I thought you might need Marguerite back." She held the doll out toward Flossie.

"Oh, Amelia." Flossie took the doll and stroked its springy curls. "I think that's one of the nicest things anyone's ever done for me." To pull herself away from rest—Flossie was humbled that Amelia would do that for her. It never ceased to amaze her that she had made a new sort of family in death. Hazel, Ada, Violet, Amelia—they all cared for one another.

She took some time straightening Marguerite's clothes and smoothing an errant hair before passing the doll back to Amelia once more. "Marguerite is yours for all eternity, Amelia. You've made me feel so much better. Thank you." She bent down to give Amelia a hug, which the girl disappeared from halfway through, filling Flossie with a feeling of content as Amelia slipped back into her dreamlike state.

Unfortunately this feeling was cut short by the air-raid siren starting up again.

"I do hope it will all end soon, Mistress Turnkey," Hazel said.

Flossie's eyes met her Advisor's. "Yes, but *how* will it end?" Her thoughts moved to the German officer. Where was he now? Reporting to his superiors with those coordinates he'd been reading out? She had to keep hunting for new information. Anything that would give her a clue as to how she might defeat him. She tapped her key against her leg, thinking.

"I'm going to go back to talk to the girl again. The one in the Invalids' Cemetery. She knows more than she's told me. I'm sure of it. Lots more."

Chapter 15

*In which Flossie returns
to the Invalids' Cemetery*

Flossie's eyes flickered open to see the Invalids' Cemetery covered in a thick blanket of untouched snow, reminding her that it was far colder in Berlin than in London. She stood quite still and took in the silent scene. The tall trees she had seen on her last visit now protectively bent their branches, weighed down by snow, over the interred, and the headstones appeared as if a sifter had been passed gently over them, leaving soft piles of powdered sugar atop them.

The girl in the white dress peered out at Flossie from behind a tree, her braids, with their bows, falling down at an angle to one side. Flossie could see that she was worried; her eyes darted around, ever watchful. Flossie would have to be careful not to frighten her off again.

"Hello," Flossie said, not too loudly in case her voice might attract the attention of the German officer. "I've come to talk to you."

The girl didn't reply.

"I've come to talk to you about what you said the last time I was here. About how this man needs to be stopped."

Still nothing. At least her eyes were focused directly on Flossie now.

Flossie waited, and eventually the girl came out from behind the tree. After some time, she took a step closer to the gates. Then another.

Flossie chose her words carefully. "I know about the skull. I know his soul is inside it," she said quietly, hoping Violet was right and that her guess would pay off.

The girl's hand moved to her mouth in shock.

Scared that the girl was about to run, Flossie spoke quickly. "Please, don't go. You told me yourself that he needs to be stopped. You said he's planning terrible things. Awful things."

There was a pause in which neither of the girls moved a muscle.

Flossie could see that the girl was waging her own war behind her eyes. She seemed to want Flossie's help but was scared. Flossie wondered what this man was doing to the interred of this cemetery. Why was this girl so afraid of him?

"I want to help you," Flossie tried again. "But I can't unless you tell me more. What's he doing? Why is he in London? Can he pass messages to the living?"

The girl took a step backward.

"No, stop!" Flossie cried out, her hands tight around the iron bars of the cemetery gates now, not caring if she alerted the Turnkey to her presence. "I can't help you if you run."

The girl paused again on hearing this truth.

"Just one thing," Flossie pleaded. "Tell me one thing." She was desperate now. "His name. Tell me his name and I'll do the rest. I promise you."

In the long silence that followed, the girl's mouth opened and closed several times until she seemed to find the courage within herself to say the words she wanted to say.

"Viktor Brun," she said, her hands clenched in fists in front of her chest. "His name is Viktor Brun."

Viktor Brun.

Flossie shook her head, thinking her ears were ringing. That she'd simply misheard.

It couldn't be.

But even as she denied it, she knew it could.

That it could easily be him.

His age. His position. The way he'd spoken her name with such disgust . . .

Viktor Brun.

It took a few moments for all of this to sink in properly. And then, when it had, it wasn't the girl behind the cemetery gates who spun on her heel and ran.

This time, it was Flossie.

Chapter 16

In which Flossie retreats

Flossie bolted down the tree-lined street, dodging piles of snow as she went. She needed to get away. From the girl. From that name.

That awful name.

It wasn't until she had run quite some way that she realized what she was doing and closed her eyes.

When she reopened them, it was the interior of a large, wood-paneled room that she saw.

She was in the Newspaper Reading Room within the British Museum. The living stood around at long desks reading newspapers propped up in front of them on wooden stands. The room had a high ceiling, and the walls were lined with books, complete with a high walkway that gave access to even more books.

Just standing in its quiet, soothing presence helped to calm her.

Flossie had visited this place many times before in both life and death, searching for articles concerning her father. Today, in the bowels of the building, it took her some time to find the volumes of bound newspapers she required. She needed to pull a copy of each one into the twilight, as well as a little cart to stack them all upon, and by the time she was done, she felt quite drained. She gathered up her strength to take the cart back to the Reading Room and to settle herself down at one of the long desks. She then started flicking through the volumes one by one.

She read the newer volumes first, because she knew all about Viktor Brun's background. Her mother had told her about him. Many times.

Because it was Viktor Brun who had stolen everything from her family.

It was Viktor Brun who had killed her father.

The two men had met at university, in England of all places, and had immediately butted heads. They had competed on all fronts — to be top of their classes, to run the fastest, to captain the rowing team, to ask out the loveliest girl. Eventually Viktor Brun had returned to Germany, but the competition hadn't ended there. Instead, they joined their countries' respective navies and then competed in a far more dangerous activity—war.

One of them was always going to win the ultimate game.

Unfortunately for Flossie's family, it had been Viktor Brun.

In 1916, the HMS *Royal Sovereign* had been Britain's newest, most expensive Revenge-class ship. It wasn't quite ready for service when the other ships in the fleet set sail for the North Sea after some important German radio messages had been decoded. The rear admiral of the *Royal Sovereign* had had reservations about the crew's readiness for battle. He had been right. Thirteen hundred men went down with the ship.

That rear admiral had been Flossie's father, and to this day he lay deep down in the dark, murky bottom of the North Sea.

It was Viktor Brun who had put him there, in that watery grave.

It was Viktor Brun who had plunged shell after shell into the thin upper armor of her father's ship, tearing it apart and sinking it immediately.

Yes, all this information she knew well. It was what Viktor Brun had been up to in the past few years that she wanted to find out. Her eyes skimming the pages before her, she learned he had joined the Nazis' feared SS elite unit in 1925. There they began to call him the Man with No Heart because he was merciless — undoubtedly why he became such a great favorite of Hitler's and one of his most trusted advisors. It seemed he had proved himself to the very end — throwing himself in front of a grenade that was meant to kill Hitler. Hitler had survived the attack on the grounds of the Berghof, his headquarters, but Viktor Brun hadn't. It had taken him a week to die.

A week that would have given him time to arrange for his soul to be captured within a crystal skull. However that worked.

Flossie closed the volume of newspapers before her and sat quite still, thinking about what she had read.

Viktor Brun, the Man with No Heart. The man

with the crystal skull. The man who had taken her father away from her.

No wonder the girl at the cemetery was scared of him.

Flossie's head sank into her left hand, her key pressing into her forehead.

It made so much more sense now. Viktor Brun was the kind of man who would do anything for his country, and here he was, attempting to win this war even though he was now dead.

What scared Flossie to her very core was that if anyone could find a way to do what had never been done before — bridging the worlds of the living and dead — it would be Viktor Brun. Sure enough, he'd find a way to pass all that information he'd been gathering to the living.

That was, if he hadn't done so already.

It also made sense as to why he'd mentioned her cemetery — perhaps that had been part of his working out who she was?

The only thing Flossie didn't understand was why he'd mentioned Hugo Howsham's cemetery as well — Kensal Green.

Over and over she repeated his name to herself.

Viktor Brun, Viktor Brun, Viktor Brun. How many times had she wondered what she would say to him if she saw him? What she would do?

Flossie's key came to life and she jumped. Someone was at the gates to her cemetery.

She was there in an instant.

"I've got news!" Ada said even before Flossie had opened her eyes again. "Apparently there's a man at West Norwood who knows what this *Ahnenerbe* is about. Come on, we've got to go and hear what he has to say."

Flossie loved visiting West Norwood—it was vast and very Gothic in appearance. She always half expected a cape-wearing vampire or two to pop out from behind one of its extravagant monuments.

When she arrived, Alice and Matilda were waiting impatiently behind the heavy iron gates, their iron key jangling on its ring as they clasped it between their hands. The ornate arched entranceway to the cemetery framed the pair in their matching white hair and shrouds. At their feet stood a large ginger tomcat with orange eyes. He was of the twilight, but quite colorful all the same. This was Old Tom, the cemetery's Advisor. He had been Alice and Matilda's beloved companion in life, and they had used his form so he might also be with them in the afterlife. Flossie saw that there was someone else with them, too. A man. A man she had never seen before.

Flossie and Ada ran to the gates, which Alice and Matilda were already unlocking.

"Hello, Alice, Matilda, Old Tom." Flossie bent down to scratch Old Tom behind the ears (he loved this).

When the sisters had locked the gates behind them once more, they got down to business.

"Now, this here is Felix Manz," Alice said, gesturing with her free hand toward the man. He was tall and lanky and, Flossie guessed, not long dead. His clothes were quite modern.

"Apparently he knows something about this *Ahnenerbe* word," Matilda added.

"A little," the man said.

He had an accent, Flossie noted—German, or Austrian maybe. She also saw that he was beginning to seem more and more unsure of himself.

"What do you know about it?" Flossie asked

as Old Tom dropped to the ground, demanding a stomach rub.

"I . . . the problem is . . ." The man halted. "Well, it's about my son. I'm not supposed to tell anyone. Not really. I won't be putting him in any trouble, will I?"

"Your son is still alive?" Flossie asked.

"Yes. He's an archaeologist."

"It's a high-ranking German officer we're interested in. Not your son."

The man visibly relaxed. "Oh, that's good."

"Tell us everything you know," Flossie said.

Chapter 17

In which Flossie returns to Germany

The man began by telling them he was Austrian, and that he and his family had been living in England for quite a number of years. His son, however, had returned to Austria after his schooling and had then studied at a university in Berlin.

"He published a lot of papers—became quite well known," he said proudly. Then his expression darkened. "And then, well, he was approached. He was offered men and money to go and search for things. Or one thing."

"Wait." Flossie held up her keyed hand. "Are you saying he was approached by the Nazis?"

The man hesitated. "Yes. They had expeditions out searching for all kinds of things. The Ark of the Covenant, Atlantis." His eyes scanned his surroundings worriedly. "It wasn't just this, though. There were other things the *Ahnenerbe* were interested in."

"What sort of other things?"

He paused. "My son had friends. Anthropologists. Sociologists. They went to places like Tibet, taking measurements, studying tribes. The Nazis—they're trying to create a new cultural history. To prove they're a superior race. They're willing to make up history to do it, too. Not only that, but the head of this division—he has other interests as well."

"Like?" Flossie pushed.

"Spiritualism. Trying to contact the dead."

Flossie stilled. So the Nazis were trying to make contact with the twilight world. The world Viktor Brun now inhabited. *And* they were searching for ancient artifacts.

The crystal skull was an ancient artifact.

"What exactly was your son sent out to search for?" Flossie focused in on the man once more, wondering if it had been the crystal skull.

"The Holy Grail," he said. "In the Pyrenees."

Flossie could barely believe her ears. Did the Nazis honestly think they could send some archaeologist out to pick up the Holy Grail? The cup that Jesus drank from at the Last Supper and that people had been desperate to find for centuries?

The man's expression became concerned. "He was beginning to worry that his time was running out. The people he was working for liked results. Fast results. They'd found many other priceless objects and—"

"What sort of objects?" Flossie stopped him in his tracks.

"I'm not sure." He shrugged. "All I know is they wanted that Grail. They had a whole room ready for it."

"A room?" Flossie said. "Where?"

"At their headquarters. At Wewelsburg Castle."

Having told them everything he knew, the man returned to rest, leaving the sisters, Ada, and Flossie standing next to the gates.

"You're going to go there, aren't you?" Ada said, speaking first.

"I think I have to. If it's the headquarters of the *Ahnenerbe*."

"You need to take that Violet lass with you," Alice said over the air-raid siren, which had just begun to wail.

"She seems to know the ins and outs of the living and their dealings with the spirit world," Matilda added loudly.

"She knew about the skull," Alice yelled. "*And* she speaks German. She can help you, I'm sure."

The sisters began to move toward the gates.

"They're right," Ada said loudly as she and Flossie followed the women. "You need to talk to Violet."

Alice and Matilda unlocked the gates, letting the girls out. After saying their good-byes and waiting until the sisters had disappeared from view, Flossie took Ada aside.

"I wasn't able to tell you this before, but I discovered something." She leaned in close to Ada so she wouldn't have to yell. "It's the officer's name. I know who he is."

"Oh?"

"His name's Viktor Brun," Flossie said. "He's . . . he's the man who sank my father's ship."

Ada drew back. "Oh, Flossie, no! Wait. What are you saying? You told me he knew your name. Do you think there's more to it? That he's here because of you?"

"No, I think it's just a coincidence, but what worries me is that it'll only make things worse. He and my father—let's just say they didn't exactly get along in life."

The drone of planes began in the distance.

"Here we go again," Flossie said.

The arched gates to Kensal Green Cemetery rose tall in front of Flossie. Towering columns loomed, as if they would like nothing better than to swallow her whole into the darkness beyond. This was a serious cemetery. A cemetery of royal burials, pomp and ceremony, and much importance. It wanted you to know that. Flossie almost felt that she should curtsy.

She walked toward the huge iron gates, which encased the smaller gates for the dead. She wasn't looking forward to seeing Hugo Howsham. Not at all.

Before she could change her mind, she rapped on

the iron gates, thinking about what Violet had said to her before leaving the meeting of the seven Turnkeys. She had said that if Flossie needed any help, she need only ask. While Flossie knew Violet would be more than willing to help in any way possible, it was her brother that Flossie wondered about.

"Miss Birdwhistle." Hugo Howsham appeared before her just as the all clear sounded. Flossie almost laughed at the timing of it. It was as if even the living, busy with their war, dare not talk over him.

"Oh, hello, Flossie." Violet approached the gates. "Have you learned more about your officer?"

"Yes," Flossie said. "I have a name now—Viktor Brun." She considered revealing Viktor Brun's link to her family and then decided against it. Hugo Howsham would only twist things to make it seem as if all of this trouble were her fault somehow. "There's more, too," she continued. "It seems that this *Ahnenerbe* group is involved in trying to contact the twilight world. I've found out where their headquarters is in Germany, and I'd like to go there. I was hoping Violet might consider coming with me."

Hugo Howsham would say no; she knew it.

Violet turned to her brother—tall, dark, and

imposing in his finely cut coat and top hat. He twisted his walking stick in the gravel, as if about to stalk away. Then he stood his ground.

"She is taking advantage of you, Violet. Haven't you learned anything in death?"

"Hugo!" Violet said. "That's not true."

"Isn't it?" he said between clenched teeth. He strode the short distance to his sister, towering over her. "She is asking you to do her job for her. I knew no good could come of a child Turnkey at Highgate, and here we are."

If Flossie could have blushed, she would have. She was glad she hadn't told him of Viktor Brun's link to her father.

Violet wouldn't be put off. "I must go, Hugo," she said. "You know this officer was talking about Kensal Green. Not to mention that the fate of our entire country could be at stake."

Flossie grinned. Oh, Violet was clever: she knew exactly how to persuade her brother. Hugo Howsham wasn't only a Turnkey who would do anything to protect his cemetery. He was also a very Victorian man with a very Victorian outlook. The fate of his beloved country was of the utmost importance to him.

"I'm practically fluent in German and used to being in an awakened state. I'll be fine if it's only a short journey. Surely I can be of help. It would be ridiculous of me *not* to go."

Hugo Howsham stood silent and still for some time, then sighed, clearly worn down by his sister. "All right. As you wish."

Flossie started. Something about his sudden change of heart didn't seem right. She opened her mouth to question his decision, then closed it again. She'd gotten what she wanted. It was probably best to leave it at that, despite her reservations.

Hugo Howsham glared at Flossie, his expression hard. "You must both be careful. Gather what information you can, but under *no* circumstances must you let this man see you. Do you understand my terms?"

"Yes," both Flossie and Violet replied.

Hugo Howsham deftly unlocked the smaller gates for the dead. Violet exited and, under the Turnkey's watchful eye, Flossie took Violet's hand in her own and thought of Wewelsburg Castle, hoping that just the name of the place would be good enough to travel by. It had worked for traveling to the Invalids' Cemetery.

When Flossie's eyes flashed open, she and Violet seemed to be standing at the end of a stone bridge that led to the immense gray castle, dark and foreboding above them with huge circular towers at each end. Crows called out from the trees overhead, which reached out black, spidery fingers into the sky. Close by stood a guard in a long gray-green wool coat. He was protected from the elements by a guardhouse that matched the castle — round with an arched doorway. His breath was visible in the icily cold night. A German shepherd stood obediently by his side.

Remembering their promise to remain out of sight, Flossie pulled Violet close to the wall of the bridge that curved around to the left so that they were half-hidden by the guardhouse. As they took in their surroundings, it began to snow. Large flakes fell from the sky. Softly, quietly, beautifully. With the castle in the background, it should have been a magical scene, and yet it wasn't. Something about this place felt wrong. Very wrong. There was an undercurrent of bad feeling here that couldn't be ignored.

Violet, who was sensitive to these sorts of feelings, had a pained expression on her face. "This is a bad place. Terrible things have happened here." She closed her eyes, as if remembering, and when she opened them again, they seemed brighter than ever. "They tortured women here. Women they called witches. So many." She frowned, focusing on a point over the bridge. "And now, in the present, over there." She pointed. "There are huts. They're using people as slaves to rebuild the castle. All kinds of people—Jewish, Jehovah's Witnesses, gypsies, and others. I can hear their voices." She covered her ears. "They wear stripes. They carry stones on their shoulders. There's not enough to eat. Sometimes the children in the village give them bread, but it's not enough. Never enough." Violet's head moved sharply to her right. Then she turned slowly in a full circle, her eyes closed again.

"What is it?" Flossie asked.

"We're near the Externsteine. I can feel it."

"The Externsteine? What's that?"

"It's a rock formation," Violet explained. "Five sandstone pillars. It's an ancient sacred site. Very powerful. I've told you before that I could feel things ever since I was a small child."

Flossie remembered this. "That you could feel

the energy of the twilight world, but you just couldn't contact it? That no one could?"

"Yes. The Externsteine is like that. Its energy is palpable."

A glossy black Mercedes convertible, the top closed, drew up to the end of the bridge and stopped at the guardhouse. The back window of the car opened, and inside was a man dressed in a gray-green uniform, the distinctive insignia of the SS on his arm.

"Come on," Flossie said. "Let's go in and see if we can find out more."

Chapter 18

In which Flossie and Violet
learn more about the **Ahnenerbe**

Flossie and Violet followed the car along the bridge and then through a gatehouse that led into a strange triangular stone courtyard. Flossie realized the castle was formed in the shape of a triangle as well.

In the courtyard, another guard opened the door of the car, and the man inside alighted. He was tall and wore glasses, and by the way everyone around him saluted him with one arm outstretched, Flossie could tell he was important. Very important indeed.

He proceeded through a door held open by yet another guard and into the interior of the castle. He walked quickly, intent on his destination, and Flossie and Violet had to almost run to keep up. As they went, Flossie noticed the wood paneling and the carpets and tapestries upon the walls. Violet touched one of the tapestries as they passed by.

Another bad feeling—Flossie could see the horror written on Violet's face.

"This doesn't belong here," Violet said, her hand pulling back abruptly. "I think it might be stolen."

They reached a doorway and the man passed through it, but Flossie grabbed Violet and held her back in case Viktor Brun was in the room. The pair checked the area carefully. When there was no sign of him, they entered.

It was a spectacular room, circular with twelve stone pillars around the perimeter and long, thin windows on the outer walls behind. A huge round oak table sat in the middle of the room with twelve seats, punctuated by a special one—a heavy wooden oak chair. It was carved with intricate designs that included swastikas. Only this seat remained empty. The other eleven seats were already taken. The men rose, saluting the man Flossie and Violet had followed inside the castle, and he took his seat in the heavy oak chair.

Silence fell over the room.

The man turned to the person on his right and said something in German.

"He wants to know if Viktor Brun is here," Violet said. "In the room."

The man he'd asked, who was short and dark and much older than everyone else in the room, closed his eyes and began to whisper.

"Oh!" Violet gasped, hearing his words. "He's a spiritualist."

It took some time before the spiritualist opened his eyes and answered the question he'd been asked about Viktor Brun.

"He says he's not here yet," Violet translated.

"But he can't really know that. Can he?"

Violet hesitated. "Normally I would say no, but the crystal skull might mean that Viktor Brun is more able to be sensed by the living."

Flossie began to worry. "If he can sense him, won't he be able to sense us as well?"

Violet raised her eyebrows. "Perhaps, but what could he do about it?"

Flossie's eyes moved to the doorway. The spiritualist might not have been able to do anything about their presence, but Viktor Brun was of their world. "And Viktor Brun? Won't he feel us?"

"It's possible," Violet answered, her mouth set in a grim line. "There are many dead here. Can't you feel them?"

"No," Flossie said. As a Turnkey, she was only attuned to the cares and needs of her interred.

"Don't fret." Violet placed a hand on Flossie's arm. "I don't think Viktor Brun is the most spiritual of men, and I'll be able to sense him when he gets close. It does sound as if they are expecting him, though."

Flossie moved from foot to foot. "What are they talking about?" she asked Violet, who was listening in again.

"Nothing of importance," she said. "Mostly about the changes that have been made to the castle. While we're waiting, perhaps we should search through those papers. They might tell us more." Violet's quick eyes had spotted a large pile sitting next to one of the men on the table.

Flossie ran over to the spot. With a *whoosh*, she pulled the pile into the twilight. She took them back over to Violet, who sat with them on the floor, her dress pooling around her. She began to flick through the pages — each one with its official swastika on top.

Flossie hovered over Violet, though she wasn't much use since the documents were in German. She must have seemed restless, because Violet's eyes met hers. "Why not investigate? There could be something we've missed. I'll listen for anything interesting."

Flossie started out around the large circular table as the men kept talking. As she walked, she eyed each of them, one at a time, frowning as she did so. It was odd — this table. Circular, with twelve seats and situated in a room with twelve pillars. It was as if they were playing at *King Arthur and His Knights of the Round Table.*

Flossie continued around the table until she reached Violet. She watched as Violet worked her way through the papers. Flossie noticed that Violet was flicking two particular sheets of paper forward, then backward again.

"Flossie!" Violet said. "Look at this."

Violet had unfolded a very large piece of paper, which Flossie studied. She didn't need to speak German to know what she was seeing.

"Building plans?"

"Yes. On a grand scale." Violet's finger traced the outside of the plans. "Huge walls and eighteen towers around the outside. Some of the other papers say it's to be the 'Center of the New World' following their final victory."

Flossie bristled. "Fairly sure of themselves, aren't they?"

But Violet was intent on the papers again, flicking faster this time, pausing only momentarily to scan each one for information as she went, until she came upon a series of papers that saw her slow down and gasp.

"What is it?" Flossie was over her shoulder in a second. It seemed to be more building plans.

"Oh!" Violet gasped. "Oh, no. No!"

"What? What is it?" By the look on Violet's face, Flossie knew it was something terrible.

"I know why Viktor Brun mentioned Kensal Green and Highgate."

Chapter 19

*In which Flossie and Violet
visit the Hall of the Dead*

Flossie steeled herself for Violet's explanation. "These." Violet held up the drawing plans. "These are for another building. A building that will stand where St. Paul's now stands. The building they want to govern our country from."

"What?" Flossie exploded.

"And these and these." Violet passed Flossie several pieces of paper. "These are for barracks. Barracks that will be built at Highgate. And at Kensal Green. As it says, 'large, unused spaces, ideal for leveling and building on without delay.'"

"No." Flossie examined the men sitting at the table and imagined them and their twilight counterpart ruling her country. Taking over her cemetery. Disturbing all her interred — including her sister and her niece. And in that moment, she saw that it could really happen. That Viktor Brun could find a way to make it happen.

"I think we should take these papers with us," Violet said, beginning to put some of the papers into a pile. "Hugo will want to see—" She visibly froze. "Wait. I can feel him. Viktor Brun. He's here. On the floor below us, I think. But he's coming closer. Quick! We need to hide!"

Flossie's eyes searched the room. The pillars weren't wide enough to conceal them; however, several large trunks had been stacked underneath one window.

"Behind there." Flossie pointed and the girls ran as fast as they could, Violet scooping up her skirt and hiding it behind the trunks at the very last second. Violet tapped Flossie's arm to indicate that Viktor was now in the room.

He lost no time in making his presence felt, his voice belting out a barrage of German. This was more for his own benefit than anyone else's, because the living officers couldn't hear him.

Violet leaned over and whispered into Flossie's ear. "He's yelling at the spiritualist. He's angry that he couldn't sense that he was waiting downstairs."

The spiritualist didn't answer.

There was a pause from Viktor Brun, then another tirade. Louder this time. Flossie's jaw closed tight as she listened to the ranting of the Man with No Heart and wondered about all those who had faced him in life.

"He's calling the spiritualist ridiculous. Worthless," Violet continued to whisper.

Then another voice called out—a voice that shushed the living men.

Silence, then . . .

"*Er ist hier!*" the voice that had shushed everyone called out. It sounded as if a chair crashed to the floor as well. As if someone had stood in surprise. It had to be the spiritualist. So, he'd finally felt Viktor Brun's presence. There was much talking from all of the living men.

Violet strained, trying to catch what they were saying. "They're going downstairs, to something called the Hall of the Dead."

Flossie's eyebrows shot up. That sort of a name couldn't be a good thing.

After a while, Flossie could hear footsteps. The men were leaving. When it sounded as if the last person had left the room, she peeked over the top of the trunks. No one was in sight.

"We have to follow them down there," Flossie said.

Flossie and Violet kept their distance, following the men through the castle. Eventually, they started down a set of steep stone steps with an iron handrail, and then the men entered the room below.

Flossie took in the room as best she could from her position, her back pressed against the wall. She and Violet needed to stay out of Viktor Brun's line of sight.

The circular room was made entirely of stone and rose to a large dome, decorated, again, with swastikas. Beneath the dome, in the center of the room, a round pit held a flame, which flickered and danced, throwing light onto the cream-colored stone of the walls. There were twelve plinths surrounding the flame, which clearly corresponded to the twelve seats upstairs. Flossie could see they were meant to hold something important — maybe even ashes, considering that the room was called the Hall of the Dead.

Craning her neck, Flossie took a peek at Viktor Brun. He was standing close to a group of the men around a specific plinth, the crystal skull under his arm. The spiritualist placed a black velvet drawstring bag on top of the plinth and opened it.

When Flossie saw what was in it, she jolted. It was another crystal skull! One that was far, far brighter than the skull that Viktor Brun held. She immediately panicked.

The Nazis had *two* crystal skulls?

Seeing her startle, Violet caught her arm.

"Two skulls?" Flossie whispered.

Violet shook her head. "No. Don't you see?" she replied. "Oh, Flossie. I know what they've done now," she whispered. "They're clever. So horribly, terribly clever."

Flossie frowned. She still didn't understand.

"Look again," Violet said, seeing her confusion. "Closely."

Flossie tried to calm herself and view the scene before her once more. There was Viktor Brun holding his crystal skull, and there was the other crystal skull on the plinth, gleaming under the light of the flames, making Brun's seem dull by comparison and . . .

Oh.

Oh, of course.

There was only ever *one* skull.

"It's the same skull, isn't it?" she whispered to Violet. "Only Viktor Brun has the twilight copy."

"Yes. The first skull you saw deceived you because of its brightness, but they're attuned. One is linked to the other. I can feel the vibrations."

"How is that possible?" Flossie struggled to work out how they'd achieved all of this.

"Think of Hugo and his walking stick and his top hat," Violet said.

Flossie frowned again. To be honest, she preferred not to think of Hugo Howsham at all if she could help it.

"Items that are buried with the dead remain with them," Violet prodded. "You, of all people, know that."

This was true. As Violet had said, this was why

Hugo Howsham had his fancy walking stick. And how Amelia would have had a doll if her parents had buried her with one. Items of significance that were buried with the dead remained with them in the twilight forevermore.

However, things still didn't make sense.

"If he was buried with the crystal skull, and that's how he has a copy of it in the twilight, how do they have the real crystal . . . ?" Flossie trailed off as she started to put the pieces of the puzzle together. "Ah."

"Yes," Violet said. "Rather disgusting, but that's what I believe they've done."

Flossie made a face as Violet continued on with her explanation.

"I'm guessing that, sometime after his burial, the living members of this society retrieved the original crystal skull from his grave."

Flossie shuddered with the thought of it — of the living officers opening up his coffin and prying the crystal skull from his hands. "How do you think they knew that it would work? How could they even know that objects buried with a person would be replicated in the twilight?"

Violet gestured toward the spiritualist. "I very

much doubt that they did. I think that our friend here guessed and hoped that this might be the case. In life, I always wondered myself if objects buried with the dead held significance in the twilight. People have believed this to be the case for a long time, after all. Remember what the ancient Egyptians used to bury with their dead — chariots, couches, mummified cats — some of the earlier pharaohs even took their servants with them. I suppose the timing and nature of Viktor Brun's death was right to test out the skull's abilities, though I have no idea how they managed to capture Viktor Brun's soul within it."

Flossie's eyes moved back to the two skulls. One in the living world. One in the twilight.

And if she could have cried, she would have, because it was now obvious that Viktor Brun had done it after all.

He'd found a way to bridge two worlds that were never meant to be connected in any way.

Chapter 20

In which Flossie and Violet return home

Inside the domed room, the living men's voices began to rise steadily, bouncing off the ceiling with strange acoustics.

Flossie leaned in close to Violet. "What's going on?" It sounded as if they were arguing about something.

Violet listened in as the voices became even more heated, then she began to whisper as fast as she could, combining the arguing voices into one.

You're the one who put him in the stupid skull with your strange death ritual. Now get him out!

I can't get him out, you ridiculous man. He's dead. *It's only his soul that's in there.*

But all we've been able to retrieve so far is some basic information on troop movements. It's not enough. We need more.

Violet and Flossie's eyes met. So it was true. He *was* getting information through to the living. Flossie's lifeless heart sank as the voices rose again and Violet continued to translate.

What's the point of Brun following Churchill around if he can't tell us everything he's seen and heard easily?

Don't you understand that it's not that simple? There is so much noise in the skull. So much disagreement. So much distraction.

Flossie reached out and clutched Violet's arm. "The other person," she said. "The other voice I heard. The second soul."

Violet nodded in agreement, her eyes still on the men. Her hand reached out to grab at Flossie's arm. "Oh, no!" she hissed.

Flossie took in as much of the scene as she could. The living officers had quieted down and stepped away, leaving the spiritualist alone with the crystal skull on its plinth. Viktor Brun stood above the skull, both hands on top of it. The spiritualist knelt on the floor, his hands on the skull as well. When all was silent, the spiritualist began to breathe slowly, in and out.

Meanwhile, one of the living officers hovered by the spiritualist's side, notebook and pencil in hand.

For a long time, all was silent. And then the spiritualist began to murmur. At first his voice was halting and unsure, but as time passed, he began to sound surer of himself, the phrases rolling faster off his tongue.

"I can't hear what he's saying," Flossie whispered into Violet's ear, worried about being heard by Viktor Brun now that the room was so much quieter.

Violet closed her eyes, listening hard. "Something about the War Rooms and some names. Names of ships, I think."

Flossie covered her mouth, stifling a gasp. "No! Violet, we have to do something." She grabbed at both of Violet's arms. "How can we stop him?"

Violet's brow was furrowed with thought. "I don't know, I . . . I think the only way would be to sever the connection. And the only way I can see to do that would be to destroy the crystal skull in the living world."

"How? We can't destroy something in the living world. And, oh—" Flossie remembered something. "The other person!"

Violet's face fell. "You're right. If we destroy the

skull, not only would Viktor Brun's soul be lost forever but the soul of the other person, too."

Flossie knew how wrong it would be to destroy the soul of an innocent person. Without a soul, no person could ever be properly, and happily, at rest.

"I can't think of any other way to stop him," Violet said.

Flossie scrutinized the skull. It almost seemed to be alight as the flame fluttered and danced in front of it. As she watched, the spiritualist's voice began to murmur again, and the officer beside him took more notes.

More information.

They didn't have any time to waste. "Let's go," Flossie told Violet. "We've learned what we came here to find out. Now let's see what we can do about it."

It was as Flossie had said. They now knew what the *Ahnenerbe*'s mission was. They knew who was involved in it, what they were doing, and what they were capable of. They also knew that Viktor Brun could do what they had feared—he could pass messages to the living via the crystal skull.

The dead were now officially at war along with the living.

Safely back outside the castle, Violet and Flossie stopped at the end of the bridge. Flossie turned back toward the castle and caught a flash of black out of the corner of her eye. Wait, had that been . . . ? For a second she thought it might have been Hugo Howsham's coat disappearing around the castle's stone wall. She was seeing things. She needed to stop being so jumpy and concentrate. Just as she was about to speak, she noticed something in Violet's expression.

"What is it?" Flossie asked.

"I've only now put two and two together," Violet answered, moving the papers she held from one hand to the other. "Do you remember I told you about the Externsteine?"

"The rock formation?"

"Yes," Violet said. "I heard them mention it just before we left, and they also said something about the upcoming full moon. It finally makes sense to me. I think they're going to try to concentrate the connection between the two skulls and the worlds of the living and the dead by using the site during a full moon."

"Would that work?" Flossie asked.

"Unfortunately, I think it would."

Flossie wanted to slump onto the hard stone beneath her feet. She felt just the same as she had on first awakening in Highgate Cemetery when she had been told she was in charge of hundreds of thousands of interred. She couldn't do this. She didn't know how. Or what to do. Or when to do it.

"How will we know when the time is right?" Flossie asked.

"They'll wait until the moon is at its highest peak. The spiritualist will be able to tell them exactly when that is, and I'll be able to tell you. I've always been able to feel the waxing and waning of the moon, and I can feel it still, even in our world. Flossie, I think this could work well for us. If I'm right about what I think they have in mind, the crystal skull will be up high on the rock formation. It would be situated in quite a vulnerable spot."

"What do you mean?"

"Well, one good push . . ."

Their eyes met as they thought about that second person. Flossie didn't like it. She didn't like it *at all*. But if they didn't destroy the skull, how many other lives would be lost? There were no right answers to be had here. It seemed there never were in war.

"So, one push," Flossie said. "But how? How can we move an object in the living world?"

It was clear that neither of them had any idea.

"We'll think of a way," Violet said.

"We have to," Flossie replied, her gaze moving back to the hills beyond the castle. Once again, she wondered if she should tell Violet about Viktor Brun and her father. She wanted to, but still thought it would be unwise. If Hugo Howsham found out that she had a personal connection to Viktor Brun, she'd never hear the end of it.

Violet's hand came to rest upon her arm. "Let's return home," she said.

Flossie opened her eyes directly outside Kensal Green Cemetery. She tapped her iron ring upon the small iron gates set inside the larger ones for the living.

She expected Hugo Howsham to appear on the other side of the gates in an instant, and when he didn't, she became wary. Had she seen him at Wewelsburg Castle? Then she caught sight of him on a path some distance away and he shot toward them, his top coat flying out impressively behind him. Somehow, that man always seemed one step ahead.

"Miss Birdwhistle." Hugo Howsham swung his key on its iron ring into his hand and unlocked the gate to his cemetery. As he pulled the gate open for his sister, Flossie took a step back, which she instantly regretted—she hated letting him think for one second that she wasn't up to her role, even if she often felt that way herself.

"I'm afraid we don't have very good news," Flossie said, gesturing toward the papers Violet held.

"I'll explain everything to Hugo. And I'll fetch you when the full moon is near," Violet said hurriedly. Flossie understood—it was best to leave her to break the news to her brother. She would know how to handle him. "Don't worry," Violet added. "We'll work something out."

Hugo Howsham watched the pair closely, but

when he saw that no more information was immediately forthcoming, he returned to locking the gates.

"Before you go, I have a message for you," he said when he was done with the lock and Violet was standing safely beside him. "The Turnkey of Tower Hamlets was here. She said to tell you that you must go to see someone called Grace immediately. Apparently she and her sister have both been taken into surgery."

Chapter 21

In which Flossie attempts to convince Grace to live

Flossie wavered. She didn't have much time. She needed to return to Highgate and speak to Hazel, but she also wanted to help Grace.

In the end, she decided to make a quick visit to Lambeth Hospital.

Grace's twilight form was in the same corridor that Flossie had left her in. She was sitting on a chair close to the entrance to the surgical theaters. She seemed smaller than ever—her back hunched over, her gas-mask box pushed to one side. Michael was talking to her quietly. His eyes met Flossie's as she approached, and he shook his head.

"The sisters had some time together, in a ward," Michael said. He took a moment to smooth his mustache. "It seems both had internal bleeding of sorts. They went back to surgery at almost the same time. Ruth . . . she didn't make it."

Flossie's hand flew to her mouth. Oh, no. Poor Grace. "Has anyone come to see them? I heard they have an aunt nearby," Flossie said.

"Afraid not."

Flossie's shoulders sagged.

"I'll grab a breath of fresh air outside," Michael said, then paused, realizing what he'd said. "So to speak."

"Thank you," Flossie said to his departing back.

Grace's form was almost doubled over in her chair. What was it about her? Flossie was used to dealing with all sorts of people in the twilight due to her job as Turnkey, but every so often she met one who was special. Someone who she really wanted everything to work out all right for. Like Amelia.

And Grace.

"I'm so very sorry, Grace," she said, placing her hand on Grace's rounded back. As she connected with her, she was shocked to feel that Grace's presence was now much stronger in the twilight world. Flossie tensed. She couldn't let Grace do this. She couldn't let her make this choice. Not now. Not like this. She would regret it. Flossie knew she would.

It was in that moment that Flossie understood why she'd come. Why she cared so much.

It was because Grace had no one else to fight for her. Her mother was gone; her sister was gone now, too. Her father had been stolen away to war. Perhaps her aunt and cousin were also no more.

If Flossie didn't take the time to fight for Grace, who would?

Flossie thought back to her old life and how lucky she had been to have people who would fight for her. She had come close to death several times when the rheumatic fever had first hit. It hadn't been like later on, when her heart had simply given out and there had been no choice to make. With her initial illness, there had been several moments when she had had to make a decision. When she'd felt that if she wanted to, she could have closed her eyes, let go, and sunk deep, deep down into her bed for all eternity. Her mother had brought her back from that place time and time again. Talking to her. Sitting with her. She would never forget the sound of her mother's voice calling her back, cajoling her, *forcing* her to remain in the land of the living. "Which dress should I wear today, Flossie?" "Cook wants to know if you'd like beef or chicken broth today." "Which book should we read this afternoon? Come on, now. I won't start until you point to one."

"Grace," Flossie said now, moving around so she stood directly in front of her. "Look at me."

Slowly, as if the effort was almost too much, Grace raised her head.

"Grace, I know what it is to lose people you love—to have them torn away from you. My father, my sister, my niece . . . it happened to me, too. Right now, you're being asked to make a decision, and it isn't a decision to be made lightly. It might seem like following your mother and sister is the easier option, but it's not—"

The wail of the air-raid siren cut through Flossie's words, and Grace's eyes darted up suddenly. Grace grabbed the notebook and pencil Flossie had left for her and wrote as fast as she could.

You want me to live?

She wrote the words in angry, jagged letters, underlining the final word several times.

Flossie met Grace's angry expression. "Yes," she said. "Yes, I do."

Again, Grace scribbled furiously, her writing spiky and disturbed.

Why should I stay here? In this place?

The drone of enemy planes outside seemed to become louder.

Flossie had no time for this. She had to go. If she didn't find a way to stop Viktor Brun, there would only be more planes. More and more and then . . . invasion. There would be no choices for anyone—dead or alive—if Viktor Brun had his way.

Flossie struggled to think of a good answer to Grace's question because there *was* no good answer. As she tried to think of something to say, she clenched her iron key tighter in her hand.

"You should choose to live because your life matters, Grace." Flossie felt a flare of anger as a picture of Viktor Brun standing over the crystal skull came into her mind. He'd taken her father, and now he wanted to take her cemetery, her country, even Grace. Well, he had taken *enough*. Flossie wouldn't let him take one more thing. Not one. She got down onto her knees next to Grace. "Every life matters. Even more so than usual right now. Don't give yours away easily."

Grace didn't move, holding the notebook and pencil still in her hands. When she eventually went to write something, her face crumpled as soon as the pencil hit the paper.

"Oh, Grace." Flossie squeezed Grace's shoulder. She didn't want to promise her anything, but surely they would send her father to her soon. Surely he would be granted compassionate leave. Perhaps that might change her mind.

It felt like an eternity before Grace's pencil connected with the paper again.

Just go.

* * *

Flossie exited the hospital. Michael was sitting on the stairs, observing the night sky, his scarlet coat spilling out around him.

"Hello," Flossie said, her voice flat.

"Hello there." Michael took off his tricorn hat and patted the place beside him.

"I'm sorry, I have to go," Flossie said, her mind already on Viktor Brun.

"Oh, you can sit for a moment. We have all the time in the world, remember?"

If only that were true. Flossie did what she was asked and sat down.

"Grace has a good head on her shoulders," Michael said. "I think she'll make the right decision in the end."

"I hope so."

"There's nothing else you could have done or said, love," Michael told her. "For Grace, I mean. It's up to her now."

Flossie shrugged. She didn't know how to help Grace. "You know, my father was a rear admiral," she said, taking in Michael's kindly face and twinkly eyes. "Sometimes I wonder if there's any of him in me at all."

"What? Of course there is! Is he buried in your cemetery, too?" Michael asked.

"I wish he had been, but no. He was lost at sea."

In life, whenever Flossie had met anyone who had served with her father, they would always tell her of his skill as a leader. How they trusted him. How they would have followed him anywhere. Every single time she had met someone who had known him, they had told her what a courageous man he had been. Oh, she wished he were here so he could tell her what to do. He would have worked out what to say to Grace. He would have persuaded her to stay in the land of the living.

With a start, Flossie realized that she'd wasted too much time here. She had to get back to Highgate. The full moon was coming, and she had to be ready for it.

Just as she was about to get up, she felt a presence behind her — the Turnkey of Brompton. She couldn't handle explaining everything again. Especially to another Turnkey.

"Hello! And good-bye!" she called out to him as she darted down the steps and away. "I really must go."

"Hazel? Hazel!" Flossie had fled through the cemetery gates and to her Turnkey's cottage.

"Mistress Turnkey." Hazel materialized in an instant. "Is everything all right?"

"No, Hazel, it most certainly is not," Flossie replied, sitting on the small upholstered footstool, gripping her iron ring and key tight. She spent the next few minutes filling Hazel in on everything that had occurred. "Violet believes the only way we can stop Viktor Brun from delivering even more harmful information is by destroying the crystal skull in the living world. But I don't see how that's possible. Even though she thinks it will be in a good position when it's taken to the rock formation, we'd have to be able to move the skull in the living world in order to destroy it, and we don't have the ability to do that."

An ominous silence filled the room.

"Hazel?" Flossie spoke slowly.

Hazel stood stock-still.

"If it's possible to move objects in the living world, you have to tell me now. Don't you understand? Highgate is at risk. Our country is at risk!"

Hazel's eyes slid to meet hers. "Mistress Turnkey, there are things you are not meant to know about the Magnificent Seven. That no Turnkey is meant to know. There is information that I am not at liberty to divulge."

"Hazel"—Flossie's voice had a warning to it— "how can you not tell me if you know something? You're supposed to advise me. Remember?"

"I do apologize, Mistress Turnkey. But to part with this knowledge could put Highgate at just as much risk as you are suggesting it is already facing."

Flossie couldn't believe her ears. Hazel knew the way out of this mess and was deliberately withholding information that might well save the cemetery and all those within it from devastation. Not to mention their city. Their country, even!

Flossie crossed her arms. "So that's it, then. You won't tell me."

There was another long pause before Hazel spoke again. "I will say no more other than that there is one person in the twilight who is privy to this information."

"And who would that be?"

Hazel's golden eyes bore into those of her mistress. "The Turnkey of Kensal Green."

Chapter 22

*In which Flossie confronts
Hugo Howsham*

Flossie stormed out of her own cemetery, away from Hazel. Her Advisor's cryptic answer infuriated her but didn't surprise her—things often worked this way in her cemetery—Highgate had always been full of dark shadows, whispers, and secrets.

This could sometimes be *most* annoying.

So intent was she on rapping on the gates at Kensal Green that she startled herself by arriving there with her nose pressed almost to its iron bars. She retreated a fraction and then tapped away insistently with her iron ring.

Hugo Howsham attended to her tapping within seconds, Violet by his side. When he saw who was at the gates, he glared that ever-present glare of his. As usual, his Advisor was not with him. Flossie knew he had brought forth his Advisor in the form of Princess Sophia, who was buried within his cemetery. Hugo Howsham's Advisor had a low-key role. It was so like him to think he knew it all. And also so like him to think he was fit company for a princess.

Oh, how she despised him.

"Miss Birdwhistle," he said, acknowledging her.

Flossie didn't care for formalities right now. She concentrated on Violet. "Apparently your brother knows a way to move objects in the living world. Did you know that?"

Violet frowned, turning to her brother. "Hugo?"

But Hugo Howsham wasn't interested in explaining himself to his sister. Instead, he unlocked the gates to his cemetery, then took two long steps to tower over Flossie, forcing her to withdraw so her back pushed into one of the entrance's high columns.

"Hugo!" Violet rattled on the locked gates, trapped inside the cemetery. "What are you doing? Stop that at once and —" Her words were drowned out by the air-raid siren's whine.

Flossie squared her jaw. She had to appear as if

she weren't scared of him, despite the fact that she always had been and he knew it. She had to show him that she was a worthy Turnkey. A Turnkey of a cemetery just as important as his. A cemetery that was just as at risk as his.

Hugo Howsham used the rise and fall of the siren to mask his words. "I saw those building plans — the plans for the barracks at Highgate and Kensal Green." He brought himself to his full intimidating height. "And I agree with Violet. The skull must be destroyed."

Flossie's eyes bored into his. "Well, then, how are we going to do that? It seems you're the one with all the information here."

He laughed then. "Plucky, aren't you?"

Flossie didn't know how to reply.

"I will help you if you require, because I must. But only when the time comes."

"So you *do* know a way to move objects in the living world?" Flossie said.

His mouth twisted, amused. "Now, I never said that. I only said I would help you if required. Until then, you must promise that you will not speak of my involvement. To anyone. Is that clear?"

Annoyed at another cryptic reply, Flossie didn't answer him, tilting her chin farther.

He moved back a tad, giving her some space, and his expression changed. "All I can tell you is that when the time comes, you will know what to do, and I will help you to do it. It is most important that you don't reveal anything about this. *Most* important."

What did he mean? Flossie caught sight of a slight vulnerability in his eyes. Was this something to do with Violet? She wasn't sure.

"I don't understand. Why can't you tell me? Why can't you explain?"

His eyes flashed with anger then. "Because I cannot. And that will have to be good enough for you if you wish for my assistance." He paused. "Is it good enough, or should we part ways right now?"

Still not willing to give the man what he wanted, Flossie offered up a shrug.

He took this as her agreement. "Violet will tell us when the time is right," he continued. "Until then, Miss Birdwhistle." He bowed slightly and headed back to the gates, which he unlocked swiftly, already flicking Violet's concerns away with a shake of his keyed hand.

* * *

Flossie gasped when she saw the view from the Golden Gallery. She had retreated there in the hope of finding a quiet place to think. It was anything *but* quiet. Smoke filled the sky, and London below was dotted with flames, the horizon of the city ablaze. Searchlights roamed the hazy sky, ready and waiting for enemy planes. In the distance, a searchlight homed in on a plane and an ack-ack gun opened fire.

And beneath that noise something else. A low drone.

Louder.

And louder still.

Flossie took a step back and watched as the planes passed overhead. She remained transfixed as the scene played out before her: the flashing of the incendiary bombs, the tearing apart of buildings, the grinding machinery of the planes, the flames whipping the air.

She moved up to the ornate iron railing, anger flaring inside her. Anger at Hugo Howsham. Anger at Viktor Brun. Anger at this stupid, senseless war.

"Stop it!" she screamed. "Just stop! Stop it now!"

She was being ridiculous. She knew it. She was screaming at nothing and no one. The living couldn't hear her, and even if they could, they wouldn't listen to her anyway. She was just a child, and a child of the twilight at that.

With the planes gone, a brief reprieve saw her eyes roam the heavens for answers.

And then she found one.

There. There in the night sky.

One single small, lonely star.

For some reason, the star reminded her of Grace, who, in turn, reminded her of her interred. All those people she had been entrusted to care for at Highgate. She could see their faces. Knew their names. Cared for them all.

And right now she felt powerless to protect them. Another Turnkey held all the cards. A Turnkey who had always despised her.

Flossie sank down the wall onto the floor below.

Now more than ever, she couldn't let Highgate down. She had to make sure that skull was destroyed before Viktor Brun's soldiers trampled their way into her country and her cemetery.

Flossie simply couldn't imagine it—St. Paul's gone. Kensal Green and Highgate cemeteries flattened to make way for armies of men.

It would be terrible enough for her interred, but the living, all those people below . . . All those Londoners . . .

To be honest, she hadn't given them much thought until now. After spending so long as a Turnkey, she felt as if she barely knew them.

She knew what they had to do, of course, each time that air-raid siren wailed—take to their Anderson shelters in their back gardens, run to the Underground shelters far below the city. Caught up in her own little world at Highgate, she had never seen it. Never seen what they were going through—the fear in their eyes. The not knowing.

Maybe she should see that, she thought.

Maybe she should see *them*. See the people she was begging Grace to remain with.

Flossie closed her eyes then and thought of the steep escalators of Piccadilly Circus station.

* * *

"Oh!" was her immediate reaction. Deep down in the Underground, she hadn't expected to see what she did—people had set up camp all over the steep escalators. Children slept; people chatted. A woman knitted a long sock. A girl read a book. A man read a newspaper, the headline LONDON CAN TAKE IT! jumping out at her.

She picked her way through the crowd, wandering toward the sound of a violin that wafted from one of the platforms.

On the station platform itself, she was greeted with yet more people, sandwiched between suitcases. Some had blankets and pillows; some did not. Some dozed, fully clothed in suits and ties, hats on their heads. Some sat, their backs against a curved wall, and listened to the man and his violin. A baby cried and was soothed by its mother.

Flossie watched them—all these Londoners—for some time. She hadn't expected this. No one quivered in fear or seemed panicked. They went about their business, uncomplaining, tired more than distressed. As if they knew they must simply bear this to get through to the other side.

This was what got to her—that they believed there would be a life on the other side of this war.

They were like that star in the sky—like Grace—faint but still shining, despite everything.

Seeing them gave Flossie a sudden burst of faith. And hope. If they could do this, she could, too.

She wouldn't give up now, or be put off by Hugo Howsham.

So, Hugo Howsham wanted to keep secrets? Well, she had a secret as well. He still had no idea about her personal connection to Viktor Brun. Maybe that was something she needed to explore in greater depth. After all, the more she knew about what was going on here, the more likely she was to find out something that might be of use.

Chapter 23

In which Flossie turns to her father

Flossie appeared atop a high cliff. Down below, the wintery North Sea crashed and rolled, booming as it hit the jagged rocks. A fierce wind buffeted the tiny tufts of plant life that could be seen through the snow. Flossie stood steady in the twilight, impervious to it. She stared far out to sea at the white-tipped waves — her father's domain.

So this was the place it had all happened — those events she'd read about so many times. The Battle of Jutland had been the strangest of battles, with each side claiming victory. The British had lost almost twice as many ships and men as the Germans, but had then controlled the North Sea for the rest of the Great War. However, Flossie saw it only as she saw this war. There were no victories. No winners. Everyone lost. Over and over again, as relentlessly as the waves crashed onto the rocks beneath.

The upcoming confrontation with Viktor Brun looming over her, Flossie could think of nothing she needed more right now than her father's advice. She had no idea how she was going to defeat Brun, and only the sketchiest promise of help from Hugo Howsham to fall back on. She also knew she didn't have the power to awaken her father and wouldn't want to do so even if she were able to. It was wrong for a Turnkey to awaken the dead from rest unless absolutely necessary. She would simply have to wait and hope that he might sense her.

Flossie closed her eyes and began to think of her happiest memories of her father. Their time together had been short. Even before he was taken from her, he had always been torn between his family and the ocean. However, the memories she did have she treasured, and they came to her mind vividly now. Walks in Hyde Park and boating on the Serpentine. An outing to the seaside where their beach chairs kept being blown away — her father cursing the wind and then laughing at the futility of it all. The time a squirrel had somehow found its way into their house and she had seen her father panicked for the only time in her life. Flossie laughed out loud remembering that and opened her eyes.

And there he was.

Resplendent in his dark-blue uniform with its shiny gold buttons — tall and solid and, oh, so very real.

Flossie's mouth opened, ready to say all the things she hadn't been able to say for so many years. And then she found she didn't have any words at all, so she ran into his already open arms instead.

The pair clasped each other tightly. But beneath the happiness of being together once more, Flossie could feel an undercurrent pulling as strong as the North Sea below them. It would have been possible to talk for days about all that had passed since they had last seen each other. But she could feel him being called back to the sea. Back to his men. He might not have been a Turnkey, but he commanded his men even in the twilight world. His men needed him more than Flossie did — they were already asking him to return.

She pulled back then.

"You're a Turnkey! And taken too young, of course. How beautiful you are," her father said, smiling down at her, "and how much I have missed you. Though you are always with me, you know."

"I know," Flossie said. "I also know you have to go, Papa, but there's something I need to ask you before you do."

"Azure," her father replied, with a laugh. "You came all this way to ask me that?"

Flossie chuckled. As a small child she was always insisting her father tell her his favorite color, and the answer was forever a shade of blue. A shade of the ocean. She was amazed at how many shades there were. He never failed to come up with a new one for her: celeste and cerulean, teal and turquoise, verdigris and viridian.

"I'm a little older now, Papa," she said. "No, it's about Viktor Brun."

A dark shadow instantly passed over her father's face. "Viktor Brun? What about him?"

"He's now of the twilight, but he's found a way to try to win the war by passing messages from the other side."

"Why does *that* not surprise me?" Her father harrumphed. "That odious man."

"I have to stop him," Flossie continued. "I was thinking the more information I have the better, and I was hoping you might be able to tell me more about him. Does he have a particular weakness? Anything that would be useful for me to know? I remember you knew him from your university days."

"That's right. From Oxford. You know, I detested him at the time, but the truth was we were very alike in many ways."

Flossie recalled the fear in the girl's eyes at the Invalids' Cemetery, Viktor Brun's ranting and raving at Wewelsburg Castle. Surely Viktor Brun was nothing like her father.

"You might think he's not like me, but the fact of the matter is that he's just a man, like all men. And just like me, his weak point will be easily located."

Flossie waited for her father to tell her the wise words that would help her defeat this man.

He leaned down and kissed her on the forehead. Flossie savored the moment. He moved back again and their similar eyes met.

"His weak point, my darling, will be his family."

Chapter 24

In which Flossie goes home

After her father's departure, Flossie stood on the cliff top, the wind whipping around her. She tried to work out how her father's advice might be useful, but couldn't see a way. She didn't know anything about Viktor Brun's family. And even if she did, she couldn't harm the living and didn't want to anyway.

Eventually, she returned to Highgate and her cottage. She ducked around the back of the cottage, trying her best not to be seen. She wasn't fast enough, however.

"I have been waiting for some time now!" Mrs. Gough's voice rang out as Flossie closed the door behind her. Flossie then proceeded to do something she rarely did — she sent Mrs. Gough to rest by force. She simply couldn't deal with her problems right now.

Flossie plopped in one of the armchairs with a thump, her head falling into her hands. She was a terrible Turnkey and she felt useless. Powerless. What was she supposed to do? Sit and wait until Violet told her it was time to go to the rock formation? And then what? Wait again for Hugo Howsham to "help" her if he deigned to?

No.

It wasn't good enough.

She wasn't good enough.

Maybe this was the end for her. She couldn't seem to sort this problem out. Perhaps it was time to ask another Turnkey to come forward. Someone older. An adult who could make better, wiser decisions.

Despite the fact that she could no longer feel physical pain, simply the thought of giving up her role felt like a blow to her chest. She couldn't bear to think about Highgate going on without her. Of another Turnkey in her cottage. Of Hazel taking another form. Of never seeing Ada or Violet again.

Overwhelmed, she brought her hands up to her face.

"Hazel!" she called out, lowering her hands. She didn't want to, but she had to ask. She had to do the best by her interred.

"Mistress Turnkey?" Hazel appeared before her.

"I want to return to rest. No, that is, I don't want to; I think I have to. I'm not sure I'm doing the right thing by Highgate. That I'm making the right decisions."

Hazel didn't flinch. "You are the chosen Turnkey, Mistress."

"But . . ."

"Highgate believes you are the correct person to lead us through this troubled time."

"I—" Flossie began to argue, then she stopped, because it was at that moment that she felt it. *Them.* All of them. All of her interred. "Oh!" she said, immediately exiting the cottage.

She ran toward the low brick wall opposite the building, on the other side of the gravel path. She stepped upon it to get a better view.

It was as she'd thought. As she'd felt. Every last one of them had stirred from rest and stood beside their graves. The usually silent, quiet, uninhabited cemetery was suddenly full to the brim, as more than 150,000 interred rose to attention. There was a sea of them—she had never seen such a crowd. Young and old, they wore shrouds and suits and dresses of different times and fashions.

Flossie's eyes scanned her interred for as far as she could see. Those who she couldn't see she felt through her key, whose iron strength ran through her veins. Marigold, Hugh, Agnes, Ellen, Adeline, Francis, Mortimer, and Jane. Lydia, Edwin, Stephen, Ann, Caroline, Jacob, Harriet, and Abigail.

Her twilight family.

How they knew what she was feeling, she didn't know. She could only think that after all these years she was as much a part of them as they were of her. The key and the earth they rested in connected them all. They and the cemetery were as one.

They'd pulled themselves from their happy dreams to tell her they believed in her.

Silently, Flossie thanked them for their support, touching her keyed hand to her heart. Then she asked everyone to return to rest. As they did, the most heavenly feeling washed through her, cleansing her troubled soul.

How strange, she thought, to feel so lucky to be dead.

And that was when the voice rang out, cutting through the silence.

"Things might be difficult, my girl, but there's still a queue to be seen to, you know!"

Flossie laughed out loud as she swiveled around to find Mrs. Gough—the only person still awake and now standing in the queue beside her cottage. She took heart in the fact that at least some things could be counted on. Mrs. Gough would be in that queue until the end of time.

With a shake of her head, Flossie jumped down off the brick wall. "Come on in, Mrs. Gough," she said. "It just so happens I have some time up my sleeve."

With a huff, Mrs. Gough entered the cottage, her long white shroud swishing around her.

Flossie rolled her eyes. The truth was, she wouldn't have things any other way.

Flossie's chat with Mrs. Gough didn't take anywhere near decades. When the old woman felt she was being listened to, she didn't rant and rave for quite nearly as long as she usually did.

No one left to see in the queue, Flossie stood from her armchair and went over to the cottage's small window with its diamond-shaped panes, her eyes trained upon the cemetery gates, despite the fact that she knew she would sense Violet at the gates if she came.

Hazel studied her closely from her spot upon the rug.

"I do wish I could tell you more, Mistress Turnkey, but I cannot," Hazel said simply.

Flossie sighed. "I know, Hazel." It hadn't taken her long to cease being cross with Hazel. Hazel was only doing her duty as best as she was able, the same as Flossie. The Magnificent Seven would always have its mysterious ways, and they were both small cogs within its very large wheel. If Hazel couldn't tell her what Hugo Howsham knew, it was for a good reason. "Apparently Hugo Howsham will help me when the time comes, though he won't tell me how."

Hazel dipped her head. "He has always been a man of his word, Mistress Turnkey."

Flossie might not have liked Hugo Howsham, but what Hazel said was true. In the past, if Hugo Howsham had said he'd do something, he'd always done it. Without fail. Maybe he *would* help her destroy the skull after all. It was only that she felt so powerless. . . .

Flossie looked out the window again. She was sick of waiting. "Hazel," she said. "Let's walk."

The pair exited the cottage and walked for some time in silence, Flossie leading them toward a place she often went when she needed to think. Her thinking spot within Highgate's walls was the architectural highlight of the cemetery — the Egyptian Avenue.

They soon veered left onto a wide, grand path. And there was ancient Egypt come to life before her: the huge pharaonic arch, flanked by two towering obelisks, the lotus flowers delicately supporting the four columns, two on either side of the entranceway.

Even before death, Flossie had known that the Victorians had been obsessed with ancient Egypt. She was glad they had, because this, oh, this. It was beautiful. Beautiful and somehow perfect in its decaying, timeless grandeur.

Flossie slipped inside the arch's iron gates, Hazel following behind her. She proceeded along the path until she reached the Circle of Lebanon — a small inner circle of vaults encased by a larger outer ring of more vaults, a pathway in between.

The structure had been cut out of higher ground, and on top of the inner circle of vaults remained what was left of the original mound. Here stood a magnificent cedar tree, tall and resplendent — its branches stretching out across the sea of vaults as if to shelter them. The tree was obviously hundreds of years old. Far older than the cemetery itself. It had seen everything and would see more after she was gone.

Her eyes on the ancient tree, Flossie felt much more calm. Almost as if whatever was about to happen were her fate. Just as it had been her fate to be Turnkey here.

Or maybe she was simply in the eye of the storm.

"Hazel, I . . ." Flossie began, but then her key rattled upon its iron ring in her hand. "It's time."

Chapter 25

In which Flossie sets out on her own

Violet stood at the smaller gates for the dead, clasping two of the iron bars. Her long wavy hair fell over one shoulder, cascading down her dress as her large eyes peered in, waiting for Flossie to appear. Several paces behind her stood her brother, with his usual solemn expression.

But there was something wrong.

"It's time to go," Violet said, her voice flat.

"And you're not coming with me," Flossie replied. She could see it on Violet's face, plain as day. Hugo Howsham had forbidden Violet from going with them to Germany.

Flossie's jaw clenched. It was unbelievable. For years he had done nothing but prattle on about how

Flossie wasn't up to caring for a cemetery such as Highgate, and the very second both their cemeteries were in danger, he stopped her in her tracks by holding back information *and* his sister's help!

None of this was Violet's fault. "It's all right, Violet," she told her, trying to remain calm.

"It's not all right!" Violet said. "I can help you both; I'm sure of it!"

Hugo Howsham didn't meet his sister's eyes. "Miss Birdwhistle must go alone."

"What?" Flossie and Violet blurted out at the same time.

"You're not going with Flossie?"

"No." This was, again, Hugo Howsham's only answer.

"Hugo!" Violet screamed at her brother, her hands grasping at him.

He disentangled Violet's hands from his, holding them firmly, his eyes on Flossie. "It's as I told you previously. When the time comes, I will help you, if required. This is all you need to know."

Flossie had heard enough. She bent beside Hazel, their eyes meeting, needing no words. Then she stood and unlocked the gates of the dead.

Violet spoke quickly. "They'll place the skull on a special altar," she told Flossie. "It's up high and not far at all from the edge of the rock formation. You won't need to move the skull much. You'll just need to tip it over the side into the void." She reached through the bars and took Flossie's hand. "You can do this. I know you can."

"I will. Somehow."

Hugo Howsham took his sister's arm firmly, and the pair disappeared from sight.

Flossie knew she needed to keep moving. Before she lost her courage.

Hazel held her dignified face high. "I will await your swift return, Mistress Turnkey."

Flossie found she couldn't reply. She locked the gates to the cemetery. Her cemetery. And as she closed her eyes, she tuned in to her interred. Her interred, all at rest, who were waiting patiently for her to come back.

It was midflight that she changed direction. Flossie wasn't entirely sure why she did it. She had never changed direction before—thought of one place, then another. It was as if someone had called out to her, beckoned her. So she thought not of a place, but of the voice. When her eyes flickered open, she wasn't entirely sure what she would find.

It had worked. She was standing outside the Invalids' Cemetery once more.

And there was the girl with the two long blond braids standing at the gate.

"You heard me," the girl said, relieved.

Flossie was surprised. How had the girl made herself heard? And what had happened to her? Because it was almost as if a different girl stood in front of Flossie now; this girl wasn't nervous or scared. She wasn't about to run away the moment Flossie spoke. She had somehow grown up overnight, from a child into a young woman.

"I must speak with you," the girl said. "The *Ahnenerbe*—they've found a way to get more information out of the skull, a way to concentrate the power. The connection between the skulls in the two worlds must be severed."

Flossie moved closer to the cemetery gates. "Yes, I know, but—"

"There's no time to explain," the girl said, cutting

her off. "Let's go." She passed straight through the cemetery gates.

Flossie gasped. "How did you do that?" It shouldn't have been possible. The interred couldn't pass through their cemetery's gates without a Turnkey's assistance. And it wasn't that the gates had been left unlocked. The girl hadn't even used the gates.

It didn't make sense at all.

Flossie shook her head, flabbergasted. "What . . . ? How . . . ? Wait . . ." She thought of something and immediately held out a hand as if to stop the girl. "If you can do that, can you also move objects? In the living world?" Maybe she didn't need to rely on Hugo Howsham's help after all. Maybe the girl was the key to all of this.

"Yes," she replied. "I can, but now we must go. There's no *time*. We must go now, before it's too late. Come! We need to go to Wewelsburg Castle."

Chapter 26

In which Flossie gains an ally

Flossie thought of the stone bridge.

She had expected to be greeted by the dark, foreboding castle that leaked centuries of dread and misery but was actually dropped into a scene of confusion in the interior of the castle. The girl pulled her back sharply to stand out of the way, in front of a large painting. Seconds later, several uniformed men passed by, deep in discussion in German. Viktor Brun wasn't one of their group, though the spiritualist was.

"You changed the destination I was thinking of. How did you do that?" It seemed the further Flossie got into this situation, the less she understood about what was going on. Was there nothing this girl couldn't do?

"We have to follow them. They were talking about what's going on downstairs, in the Hall of the Dead," the girl replied, ignoring Flossie's question, her eyes not budging from the doorway. "Come on."

Flossie was going to ask another question and tell her she'd visited here before, but it was too late. The girl had already started off. Talking would have to wait until later.

Just as she'd done with Violet, Flossie followed the officers downstairs. She and the girl trailed them at a distance until, once again, they came to stand in the shadows at the bottom of that set of steep stone steps with its iron handrail.

As before, the flame was alight in the middle of the twelve stone plinths. This time the crystal skull stood at the ready, its velvet bag tossed to one side. Behind it stood Viktor Brun, holding his twilight skull. He glared angrily at the spiritualist, who was talking to some of the other officers, unaware of his presence. It was obvious that his gift for sensing the twilight world wasn't strong. Certainly not strong enough to appease the demanding Viktor Brun—that was for sure.

A cloud must have shifted, because moonlight began to stream through the dome's angled windows, a beam hitting the crystal skull. Flossie drew back, shocked by the light that burst from it, filling the room.

The spiritualist shouted out in German, realizing that Viktor Brun was now present.

Everyone moved into place then—Viktor Brun lunged forward, the spiritualist knelt on the floor, his hands darting out to the skull, and another officer stood with his notebook at the ready.

Flossie expected the information to come haltingly, as it had before.

It didn't.

With a jolt, the spiritualist began to speak, much faster than last time, the officer taking down more notes than he previously had. Flossie watched as information was leaked from the crystal skull. Every so often, she heard a word or two that scared her to her very core. *Cambridge. Bath. Dover.* On and on it went as her fist clenched ever tighter around her iron ring. The words came faster and faster until she doubted how much more she could listen to before she must do something to stop them.

Then, just when she thought she could bear it no longer, the clouds moved again, the beam of moonlight disappeared, and the spiritualist ceased speaking.

"*Nein!*" Viktor Brun cried out, but only Flossie and the girl could hear him.

The spiritualist rose from in front of the plinth, seeming drained. The other officers crowded around him and a heated discussion ensued.

"What are they talking about?" Flossie asked.

"Some of them want to stay here, and some of them want to go to the nearby rock formation. The Externsteine. Do you know what that is?"

"Yes. A friend told me that might be their plan: to use the site along with the full moon to make a stronger connection between the worlds of the living and the dead. She said it would be a good place to destroy the skull. That they'd place it on an altar high up, and it would just need one good push."

"A very good idea," the girl replied, then she caught something that was being said inside the room. "Wait. They have decided. They will stay here a little longer. Until the moon reaches the full height needed for the best connection between the skulls." She gestured back up the stairs. "Come, we will wait upstairs."

At the top of the stairs, the girl moved to her right and sat down upon the stone floor, her legs tucked under her.

Flossie sat beside her, unsure. There was so much about this girl she didn't understand. Perhaps she sensed Flossie's unease, because the girl began to speak.

"You want to know why I'm here, don't you? Why I want to stop him."

Flossie nodded. She wanted to know this and so much more besides.

"The reason is simple," the girl told her. "I know what he and these men are capable of."

Flossie waited for more information.

The girl gave a small shrug. "Here, I will tell you a story." She pulled her knees to her chest and hugged them tight before she began.

"There was a girl once, just like me. Her name was

Hana. She lived downstairs from my grandparents, and I used to play with her every Sunday when I went to visit them. We liked to draw together or run around outside. My father and grandfather didn't like me playing with her very much, but my grandmother would tell them to be quiet—that Hana's parents were good people. Then, one Sunday, we went to visit my grandparents and something was wrong. My grandfather was very quiet and my grandmother was"—she struggled to find the word—"upset. She argued with my father and grandfather. She told me I couldn't go down to see Hana."

There was silence as the girl closed her eyes, remembering.

"While my father and grandmother argued, I slipped away. I ran downstairs, and Hana's family's door was open. Their possessions were everywhere, and the family was nowhere. I ran back upstairs. I could see something very bad had happened. I knew they were Polish and that they were Jewish, of course. But they had been here so long, I never thought . . ." She shook her head. "They had been sent back to Poland. They were allowed to take nothing. Nothing! Only the clothes they stood in and the very smallest amount of money." She was unable to continue.

Flossie reached out a hand.

"What happened to Hana?" she asked.

The girl only laughed a grim laugh. "How would I know? You think someone cares? Someone checked? Two weeks after this, synagogues were burned, Jewish businesses destroyed, and men beaten. Thirty thousand people were taken away! I thought then that the Nazis would be stopped. That other countries would step in. But no. No help came. None is coming. I see that now. And what I have told you is nothing, *nothing* compared to what the Nazis are planning."

Flossie waited, sensing the girl had more to say.

The girl's eyes, which had been fixed upon the stone floor, moved to meet Flossie's once more. "Even without his help, they will do terrible damage, but with his help, the world as we know it will end forever."

Flossie paused to gather her thoughts. So many questions ran through her mind that she didn't know where to start. "How have you heard all about this? By listening to him? When he's at the cemetery?"

No answer.

"I still don't understand, though. Why aren't you at rest? Why is there no Turnkey? Surely your Turnkey could help you?"

The girl waved a hand now, agitated. "The Turnkey is so afraid of Brun's strange powers that he's gone into hiding. Don't you see that none of that matters? All that matters now is that he must be stopped."

There was so much that didn't add up here. "You've changed," Flossie said. "When I first saw you, you were scared of him."

"Yes, but not anymore," she replied. "Not now that I understand all that he is capable of. I only have to think of Hana and I know that I must destroy the skull once and for all. It is the only way."

"How can you move objects in the living world?" Flossie's eyes narrowed.

There was a long pause. "I just can."

Flossie didn't like that this girl was being just as mysterious as Hugo Howsham, but she could have hugged her anyway. Anything not to have to rely on that horrible man.

"I don't even know your name." Flossie held out her hand. "Mine's Flossie."

The girl took it in hers and shook it firmly.

"Elke," she replied.

Chapter 27

In which Flossie climbs the Externsteine

Before long, the voices rose again downstairs in the Hall of the Dead.

Something was happening.

Elke told Flossie to stay where she was and retreated down the stairs. Flossie crawled around to watch her descend. Below, Elke listened in for a minute or two before returning.

"They're preparing to leave," she said.

"So," Flossie said, "this is it." All those notes that had been taken downstairs, when the moonbeam hit the crystal skull—she could only imagine the help that the light of a high full moon in the midst of a sacred rock formation would provide. The information stored inside the skull would be made effortlessly available.

Elke squared her shoulders. "We should go now," she said, as if attempting to talk herself into this. "It will take the living men a while to drive there, but we have the advantage. We can go there now and ready ourselves."

As the men started up the stairs from below, Flossie offered Elke her keyed hand.

"Oh!" Flossie exclaimed.

She had expected to see some small standing stones, the likes of which she'd seen in her own country. But this, this was an incredible sight. The pair were standing on a road that ran between several tall, narrow rocks that soared up toward the sky. The light of the moon shone white and bright, illuminating their sandstone crevices and casting eerie shadows.

Elke dropped Flossie's hand.

"Come," she said, beckoning her.

Flossie followed her along the road, the rocks towering above. After a few more steps, they came to stand in front of a large religious carving in the rock face itself, high above their heads.

Both girls' eyes were fixed upon it in awe.

"It's medieval," Elke told her. "People have been coming here for a long time. Forever, I imagine."

Flossie's attention had moved away from the carving as she recalled all Violet had told her. "Where's the altar?" she asked Elke. "I was told that's where they might place the crystal skull."

"Yes, that's right. It's up there." She pointed to the tallest of the stone towers — the one that stood by itself in the middle of the others and had to be reached via a small, rounded, iron footbridge.

Flossie found the stairs she needed and then she was off, Elke running behind her to catch up.

The stone stairs were quite wide, but narrowed as the two towers of rock came closer together overhead. Flossie paused midflight, a strange, heavy feeling coming over her. It was almost as if someone were watching her. Was Viktor Brun here already? She could see only Elke. She felt uneasy, the rocks heavy overhead. She had to keep going. Flossie started upward again, the stone steps curving around the side of the wide expanse of rock as they ascended.

The girls moved to the point that would lead to the iron footbridge.

They turned the corner, and the footbridge was before them. Flossie paused at the edge of it. It was a short bridge, rounded and exposed, and the ground felt a long, long way below. There wasn't time to be scared. One hand on each of the railings, she crossed it, her key clinking — iron against iron — as she went.

"Over there." Elke indicated the small rock alcove to their right, only a step or two away from the end of the footbridge.

Surveying the altar, Elke stiffened.

"He's close," Elke said. "I can feel his presence. This way." She ran back over the footbridge and crawled into a hiding space in the rock wall on the other side. There was just enough room for the two of them, and from here they had a view of what was going on near the altar. Above, the moon dimmed — hidden by a cloud.

It felt like hours before they heard the living officers' voices as they approached. Then they saw them — several of the heavy-coated officers tramping over the footbridge, the silver braid on their uniforms and shiny skulls and crossbones on their hats glinting in the moonlight. Flossie and Elke squashed in together even tighter when they saw the last two men pass by—Viktor Brun and the spiritualist. The spiritualist carried the black velvet bag, heavy with its precious crystal contents. Viktor Brun held the skull of the twilight world. They crossed the footbridge, the spiritualist already uncloaking the crystal skull as he went. He lost no time in placing it inside the small alcove, on the altar itself.

Thankfully, the moon was still behind a large cloud.

"How are we going to do this?" Flossie whispered to Elke. "Should I distract him while you grab the skull?"

Elke's expression was determined. "There's no rush. He'll let me near him. You'll see."

"He might know you from the Invalids' Cemetery. But does he *trust* you?" Flossie wasn't sure about this.

Elke laughed a strange little laugh. "Yes."

Flossie pulled back. There was something not quite right about this. She had a bad feeling. "Elke..." As she spoke, she saw that the cloud above was moving again. Soon the moon would reveal itself in its full glory once more.

Both the spiritualist and Viktor Brun were intent on the altar.

And that was when it happened.

The cloud passed by, the moon shone down, and the world was filled with light—the kind of which Flossie had not seen since she was alive. It was that blinding sort of light that comes from stepping out of the house on a bright summer's day. Flossie squinted and held a hand to her eyes as she attempted to make out what was going on.

When she had adjusted to the light, she noticed that the crystal skull of the living world shone brighter than she had ever believed possible. The colors emanating from it lit up the rock formations in a dazzling display. The twilight skull also shone like a beacon.

But that wasn't all there was to be seen. Now the living officers pointed at something, a range of expressions on their faces—shock, fear, awe.

As one, they pointed at Viktor Brun.

Chapter 28

In which Flossie finds out the truth

The living can see him!" Flossie whispered to Elke. "It's working. The connection between the skulls is far more powerful here. They'll be able to communicate directly." The living officers circled Viktor Brun, amazed, terrified, and talking hurriedly.

With every second that passed by, Flossie's panic rose. Soon the living officers would get over their astonishment, and they'd move on to obtaining all the information Viktor Brun could give them. That skull had to be destroyed. When Elke didn't make a move, Flossie began to get up. But Elke only pulled her back down.

"No! They'll be able to see us as well. Just stay here a moment. It's all right," she said, nodding upward as the moon passed behind another cloud.

Everything dimmed once more, and Flossie rested her head against the rock, relief flooding her body.

The men's voices rang out with confusion, the light from the crystal skull gone, as was their view of Viktor Brun.

The spiritualist's voice rang out the loudest, as if hoping to restore order.

Elke translated. "He's telling them that soon they will have all the information they need."

Everyone stared at the sky, waiting.

Everyone but Flossie, whose eyes scanned the rock formation.

She wasn't surprised that Hugo Howsham was still nowhere to be seen.

And Elke, what was she waiting for?

She'd said she wanted to destroy the skull, and now it seemed as though she was having second thoughts. Well, there was nothing else to do — Flossie would have to try to push the skull from the altar herself. Maybe there *was* a way. Perhaps the strong link between the skull in the living world and the one in the twilight world would enable her to move it? She didn't know.

She only knew she had to try.

Flossie grabbed Elke's arm. "I have to go now. I can't wait any longer. I have to try to destroy it. Don't you understand? I can't let them have that information."

"Not yet. We need to wait for them to be distracted again. Wait for the moonlight. Then we'll move. I'll run over and snatch the skull while you distract him." Elke seemed strangely calm.

Her thoughts confused and jumbled, Flossie tried to make sense of what Elke was saying. Maybe she was right. If Flossie ran now, Viktor Brun would notice her in a second. If he was distracted by the light of the two skulls, they'd have more time to carry out their plan.

"All right," Flossie agreed. Slowly, slowly, the cloud passed by until the light of the moon began to seep through the edges.

Just as the moon was about to reveal itself completely, Elke clutched Flossie's hand. Her eyes were wild, the calm of before gone. "Remember me," she said, whispering no longer. "Remember me. And Hana."

Elke pushed past her as the blinding light came once more — even brighter than before, if that was possible. Flossie held up a hand to shade her eyes for a second.

When she brought her hand down again, Elke was gone.

Flossie stood, not caring any longer about remaining concealed. "Elke!" she called out as, through the light, she saw Elke running across the footbridge. She was almost at the other side already. There, the officers were pointing again, shocked not only by their view of Viktor Brun in his twilight form but also by seeing two more people from the twilight world.

Viktor Brun, however, paid their gasps no heed. He was intent on Elke, who reached him without hesitation. When Flossie called out, she noticed that he didn't seem surprised to see her at all.

It was almost as if he had been expecting her.

Standing at the end of the footbridge, Flossie paused, unsure of what was going on.

"Ah, so you've brought her after all," Viktor Brun

said to Elke, speaking in English. He clapped his hands together as if he were pleased.

It was seeing them standing together, so at ease with one another, that brought Flossie to the awful realization of what was going on.

Elke calling to her from the Invalids' Cemetery, bringing her here, Viktor Brun's lack of surprise on seeing her — it had all been a trick.

Elke was never going to destroy the crystal skull. She'd never had any intention of doing so. This was all a trap in order to lure Flossie to this place.

"You lied to me!" Flossie boomed. "You're on his side. You always were. You *lied* to me!"

She expected Elke not to be able to meet her eyes, but Elke's gaze was level and unrepentant. She didn't seem the least bit sorry, or as if she'd betrayed her, which made the knife in Flossie's stomach twist that little bit more painfully. Flossie wondered if it had all been a lie, even the story about Hana. But no, it couldn't have been. Flossie had seen the expression on Elke's face as she'd told that tale. She had meant every word of what she'd said. Flossie had felt the truth of the words deep inside her.

Viktor Brun approached the footbridge and laughed cruelly.

"So, here she is—the girl who would protect Churchill. Protect all of Britain! How sad that she's failed just like her father before her. You know, I couldn't believe my luck when I did some research into who this strange little Turnkey on top of St. Paul's was and found that the name was one I knew well."

Flossie reached out and grabbed the iron railing. So he'd known who she was all that time.

"Come here, my *Liebchen*, my darling." With his free arm, Viktor Brun beckoned Elke even closer, his other arm holding the skull of the twilight tightly.

Elke leaned into him, flicking her blond braids to the side. He clasped her to him, and an audible gasp came from the living officers present. With his touch and the contact with the twilight skull, they could see Elke even more clearly than before. It was almost as if they were both alive again.

Viktor Brun looked down at Elke fondly. "All this time chastising me. I knew you would see reason in the end."

Finally, Flossie understood.

Darling. Chastising.

The last piece of the puzzle fell into place.

"You're his *daughter,*" Flossie blurted out. That was why Elke was able to speak English. She'd mentioned her father had been a Rhodes scholar. Flossie hadn't known that Viktor Brun was one, too, only that he'd gone to Oxford with her own father. Other things also made sense — how Elke had been able to exit the Invalids' Cemetery in the way that she had. How she had called out to Flossie. Why she said it was "impossible" that she return to rest.

It was impossible because her soul was trapped inside the crystal skull.

Which meant what she had told Flossie before was true — she *could* move objects in the living world. Because part of her soul remained there.

"*You're* the other person inside the skull," Flossie continued. Elke was the younger person. It wasn't an ancient Mayan soul at all, but Brun's daughter. Oh, how right Flossie's father had been, pointing her in the direction of Viktor Brun's family. Why hadn't she listened to him more carefully?

"I thought I'd finished with your father on the

North Sea." Viktor Brun sneered at Flossie. "Then his beloved Britain took my daughter with their bombs, crushing her chest. A slow, horrible death. However, we were lucky in some ways. A slower death gave us time. Only a month before, one of our archaeologists had located a crystal skull and brought it back to the Fatherland. When we knew Elke was unlikely to live, our spiritualist leader informed us that he believed he could capture Elke's soul within the skull by performing an ancient ritual at death. When he thought he had accomplished this, he then did the same for me when I suffered my fate. It was then that he came up with yet another brilliant idea — to bury the skull with me and then retrieve it in the hope that we might forge a connection between the worlds of the living and dead."

So it was as Violet had guessed. They'd buried the skull with Viktor Brun and then dug it up again.

Viktor Brun saw Flossie's expression. "You feel ill at ease with my decision? This is nothing compared to what is coming. Your country took my daughter from me — now it's *my* turn for revenge. And what a lovely place your little cemetery will make for soldiers' barracks. How your father would have hated that—enemy barracks built on top of his daughters' and granddaughter's graves! There is nothing you can do about it. Don't you see it's pointless, your coming here? You can't stop us now. You can't touch the crystal skull in the world of the living. It's beyond you. Ah, it will be pleasing to see those barracks built. And *my* daughter will be able to watch the spectacle with me. Together forever." He grinned at Flossie wolfishly. "Don't you wish your father had had access to such artifacts as our crystal skull?"

At any other time Flossie would probably have taken his bait, but something nagged at her— something that still didn't make sense.

When Flossie had touched the twilight skull at the War Rooms, she had felt that fierce argument between the pair going on inside it. It was the sort of battle that was heartfelt and not to be backed down from. What she'd felt—it was Elke to the very core. Just as Flossie had known the story about Hana was true, she knew this was true as well.

And that was when Elke began to edge away from her father.

Chapter 29

In which Flossie discovers Elke's plan

Elke whirled into action, snatching the twilight skull away from her father and departing from view with it. The light surrounding the officers and Viktor Brun dimmed with the twilight skull's disappearance, though the crystal skull of the living world still shone strongly upon the altar.

When Elke appeared again, it was in front of the altar, and the two skulls shone like stars, making everyone present — both living and dead — wince. She placed the twilight skull upon the rock wall and then went to take the crystal skull.

It wouldn't move.

She pushed and pulled at it, obviously desperate to get it over to the rock wall.

And still it wouldn't budge.

Flossie couldn't believe what she was seeing.

Elke *had* brought her here to destroy the skull after all.

What was wrong? Maybe she couldn't move objects in the living world as she'd thought.

Viktor Brun watched his daughter's actions, his jaw set hard. "The crystal skull cannot be harmed by those inside it," he told Elke, calm and controlled. "It preserves itself. Though I'm not sure why you would want to damage it. Do you have any idea what you're doing?" His voice was stern.

Elke's expression became panicked. She looked to Flossie for a split second, then picked up the twilight skull once more and clutched it to her.

Then, in the blink of an eye, she was gone.

Viktor Brun stood perfectly still, his fury simmering.

It was one of the officers who spotted Elke first—alerting them all to her location by pointing at the next rock tower over, where a bright light now shone. There was Elke—standing by herself.

Viktor Brun stood at the edge of the rock tower and faced his daughter.

"Elke, we have business to attend to!" he yelled. "Return immediately."

Elke didn't reply.

"You must stop this *now*, Elke!" Viktor Brun had had enough. He stamped a foot in frustration.

"No!" Elke called back, her voice unwavering. "No. I won't stop. It's *you* who has to stop. How can you do these things? Plan these things? Why did you get that horrible man to put me inside the skull?"

The spiritualist, who had returned to Viktor Brun's side, now inched away from him nervously.

"I hate the skull. I *hate* being inside it," Elke continued. "I hate knowing what I know. Knowing what you're planning. What you're thinking. When I was little, I thought you were good and kind, but now I can hear your every thought and I know you're not. You're not! I thought someone would come and stop you. It was only when Flossie arrived that I realized it had to be me. That *I* had to stand up to you."

"Elke . . ."

"Enough!" Elke replied. "I won't do what you say anymore. I don't trust you. How can you do those things to other people—to people like Hana—and then still love me? I don't understand it. The things you're planning, they're evil. Pure evil."

"Elke! Get back here now!" her father screamed at her. "You will *not* disobey me."

"I won't come there. I'll only talk to you if you come here. I don't want to talk in front of all those men."

Viktor Brun was gone in a flash.

Flossie was too far away to see Elke's face, but there was something in her stance—determined and fierce—and it was directed at Flossie. It was then that Flossie realized this was it.

This was their second chance to destroy the skull. Elke was providing a distraction.

But if Flossie destroyed the crystal skull, Elke would be gone forever. With no soul, she could never be at rest. She would cease to exist on any plane.

Flossie couldn't do that to her.

She couldn't!

The voice came then, clear in Flossie's head.

You have to, Flossie. Please. Do it for me. And Hana. For your interred. For all of us.

From their opposite stone towers, the girls faced each other as Elke's father appeared beside her.

This was it. It was now or never.

The only problem was, Flossie had no way of doing what Elke asked.

Still, she had to try.

Flossie closed her eyes and appeared near the altar and the crystal skull. She jumped as she realized that there was a man standing next to her. A tall man dressed all in black.

Hugo Howsham.

"Give me your hand." He spoke quickly, taking her keyed hand in his so that their two iron rings clinked together. His eyes met hers. "Now take it from me. Take my key. The skull must be destroyed once and for all."

"I don't . . ." Flossie began, but then it happened all by itself. As if by magic, his key appeared on her ring and the words came, unbidden. "I am the Turnkey of Kensal Green; the dead remain at rest within." At the same time, the strangest feeling came over her. A rush of names and faces and cemetery plots — not of those interred at Highgate, but at Kensal Green.

And something else, too. A new sort of strength. A powerful feeling.

Amazed, Flossie's eyes met Hugo Howsham's. But there was no time to question him as the living officers began to approach them, yelling in German.

Now. Now! Please, for all of us. Now! Elke's voice came again.

As the living officers closed in, Hugo Howsham stepped between them and Flossie moved into action. She ran over and reached for the skull, the awful turmoil of Elke's and Viktor Brun's conflicting souls screaming out at her as she made contact with its smooth surface.

"Now!" Hugo Howsham yelled as Viktor Brun, sensing the impending danger, appeared back on the top of their rock tower.

Focusing her newfound power, Flossie heaved the skull to the edge of the rock wall as Hugo Howsham wrestled with Viktor Brun.

There was no time for hesitation. As the men clashed, she moved the skull into position. Then, just as she felt one of Viktor Brun's hands grip her shoulder, she pushed the skull with every ounce of strength she had left, and it slid off the rock wall.

It fell toward the earth, tumbling, shining, shards of light twisting and twirling as it went.

Down.

Down.

Down.

"You stupid girl," she heard Viktor Brun say, his voice dripping with hate.

Hugo Howsham moved between them again and gave Viktor Brun a hard shove backward, releasing Flossie. Brun landed at the feet of his officers as his daughter appeared before him.

Thank you, Elke said silently, her eyes shining at Flossie. *Thank you.*

The crystal skull connected with the hard, wintery ground.

As it broke into a million dazzling pieces, there was a final burst of brilliant white light from both skulls. A light so blinding that Flossie had to cover her eyes with her hand and its two keys.

When she lowered it once more, Elke was gone.

And so was Viktor Brun.

Chapter 30

In which Flossie and
Hugo Howsham make amends

Flossie's eyes were fixed upon the space where Elke had been standing.

She was gone.

Elke was gone.

Her soul had been destroyed along with the crystal skull. Destroyed along with her father's soul. They were no more.

Flossie was in awe of how brave Elke had been. There were grown men who cowered in the presence of Viktor Brun, but it was a young girl—his own daughter—who had stood up to him when no one else would.

The scene now lit only by the light of the moon, there was stunned silence from all present on top of the stone tower—living and dead. That is, until, as one, the officers started shouting and arguing. Only the spiritualist remained quiet—slumped upon the stone floor, looking utterly defeated.

Flossie, knowing they could no longer see her, ignored them all, intent on that spot where Elke had stood.

She'd do as Elke had asked. She'd always remember her. And Hana. She'd *never* forget what Elke had done, how many lives she'd probably saved by sacrificing herself and her father, whom she obviously loved, despite his faults.

Flossie felt something strange and wet on her face. At first she didn't understand, but when she did, she gasped, bringing her fingers to her cheek.

She was crying. She could *cry.*

Shocked, she lifted up her keyed hand. The two keys had not only given her the power to hurl the crystal skull from the top of the rock formation; they'd also given her the ability to cry as the living did.

"Oh!" Her hand shot to her chest as she detected something—the very faintest of heartbeats.

Hugo was leaning against the rock wall. "So," he said. "Now you know." He pushed himself up off the wall, appearing drained. "I'll have my key back now, if you don't mind."

"Of course," Flossie said. She couldn't help but notice how nervous he was. Almost as if he thought she might not give his key back. She'd never seen Hugo Howsham nervous before. He knew that he'd given her the opportunity to be more powerful than he. To hold all the cards.

Flossie offered him her iron ring. He brought his own ring together with hers and another strange feeling swept over her—those same names and faces being stripped from her as if she were a tree being uprooted from solid ground. That power was taken from her, too. There would be no more tears. No more fluttering heartbeat. She heard Hugo Howsham's voice as if from afar.

"I am the Turnkey of Kensal Green; the dead remain at rest within."

Flossie had to sit down—only one key jangling upon her iron ring once more. Hugo Howsham assisted her, catching her elbow and lowering her to the stone floor.

"I am sorry," he said gruffly. "It's not the most pleasant feeling." He knelt beside her. "Now do you understand why the other Turnkeys must never know?"

"I had a heartbeat and I could cry. If I could do all of that with two keys, what would happen if—?"

"These are questions that are best not asked," Hugo Howsham said, cutting her off. "This is why I didn't come with you to this place. Why I've stood back and watched this whole time. I was hoping that you would find another way to destroy the skull. You almost did. But there was no other way, as it turns out. Now you know what we were never meant to know and what you must never tell the other Turnkeys. You must promise me you won't tell them. I should never have known myself that the keys could be combined. I found out by mistake and . . ." He looked away. "Sometimes I am sorry that I did."

Flossie frowned. "What do you mean? How did you find out?"

"No more questions!" Hugo Howsham bellowed. "The Magnificent Seven never meant us to have this information, and we must act as if we don't. As if we never knew at all. Are we agreed?" He offered her a hand up.

Flossie took it and rose. "I . . ." she started, not quite knowing what to say. She didn't understand. Not at all. But, strangely enough, she trusted his judgment on this. She could see how if this knowledge fell into the wrong hands, terrible things might happen. "Yes," she answered him. "I won't tell them."

"Good."

She remembered something. The flash of black at Wewelsburg Castle. "You followed us, didn't you? The first time I visited Wewelsburg Castle with Violet."

He dipped his head. "Perhaps."

"You did! I saw your coat."

"I wasn't sure you were up to the task."

She remembered something else. "I didn't want to tell you before, because . . . well, I was worried that you wouldn't help me if you knew. Viktor Brun — he was the man who killed my father. Who sank his ship. Who took his men."

Before he could reply, their attention moved to the German officers, who seemed to have worked out that the rock formation was useless to them now. After some discussion, two of them dragged the spiritualist to his feet and they retreated, crossing the iron footbridge and leaving Flossie and Hugo Howsham on their own.

Hugo Howsham cleared his throat, his attention moving to the moon above.

"I'm afraid I've said and done some rather foolish things, Miss Birdwhistle." He ground his walking stick into the stone.

"Oh?" Flossie replied.

His green eyes moved back to her then, clear and true and very much like his sister's. "I was wrong about you, and I'm sorry for it."

Flossie hadn't expected such a direct apology.

"That's all right," she said. "I understand." And she did understand. Being a Turnkey was difficult. She rarely thought she was making the right decisions. If Hugo Howsham returned to rest and someone her age were given the task of caring for Kensal Green, she knew she'd be dubious about their abilities, too.

As a feeling of peace settled between them, Hugo Howsham took in their surroundings — the small rock altar, the rock towers, the lake in the distance. "What a strange life we have," he said. "Or death, should I say?"

Flossie couldn't help but agree with him. "Death is a strange place, Mr. Howsham," she replied. "I thought it was supposed to be all pearly gates and fluffy white clouds and angels, and it's not. There's a lot no one ever told me about in Sunday school — *that's* for certain."

He laughed a short laugh at this and then bent down slightly to offer her his arm.

"Home?" he said.

"Home," Flossie replied.

Chapter 31

In which Flossie returns to London

Hugo Howsham returned to Kensal Green. Flossie stopped at both Tower Hamlets and Highgate to let Ada and Hazel know she was all right and that the skull had been destroyed. She didn't say exactly how this had happened. Hazel knew, of course, though she led Ada to believe that it had been Elke who destroyed it.

She hated lying to Ada. Hated it. But she knew that Hugo Howsham was also right — the power of combining keys was dangerous and could easily be abused. The fewer people who knew about it, the better.

Flossie's visit to Ada was brief, as her mind was focused on another place she needed to go.

Flossie opened her eyes in a familiar corridor of Lambeth Hospital. She had to speak to Grace. Elke hadn't been able to help Hana, but Flossie was now more determined than ever to see Grace through her troubles and to convince her to live.

"Grace?" Flossie called out amid the hustle and bustle of the busy hospital. She stepped to one side as a patient was wheeled hurriedly past her toward surgery.

When she couldn't find Grace anywhere, Flossie began to lose heart. Then Michael appeared at the far end of the corridor, his tricorn hat tucked under his arm. The Turnkey of Brompton was with him.

"Everything all right?" the Turnkey of Brompton asked.

"Yes, in a way," Flossie replied, her voice tired and drained. "The skull is gone forever. I'll explain it all to you. Sometime."

The Turnkey of Brompton seemed to understand.

"Come on, then," Michael said, gesturing. "This way. Her ward's over here."

"Has Grace . . . ?"

"No, love," he answered. "Part of her is still here with us, as before. I see that as a good thing. There were times I thought she was close to letting herself slip away from life and stay with us forever. To her credit, she didn't. She's strong, that one."

Flossie hoped that Grace had taken to heart some of what she'd said at their last meeting.

Michael moved toward the stairs and Flossie followed, the Turnkey of Brompton close behind them. "She's up this way. She's been sitting by her own bed. I can't be sure, but I think she's close to making a decision, and I'm hoping it'll be the right one."

"I hope so, too," Flossie replied, following him. "I really hope so."

Upstairs, it was just as Michael had said. In among the many beds, full of people affected by bombing in one way or another, there was Grace. She sat upon a small stool that had been left by her bedside, watching over her sleeping self.

As Flossie approached Grace's bed, she drew another stool into the twilight with a *whoosh* and carried it over with her.

"How about we leave you ladies alone for a bit?" Michael said. And with a dip of his head, he and the

Turnkey of Brompton left the way the three of them had come.

When Flossie reached Grace, she placed the stool next to her.

"Mind if I sit down?" she asked.

Grace's twilight form seemed surprised to see Flossie. She pushed her gas-mask box to one side and brought out the small notebook and pencil Flossie had given her. She began writing.

I'm sorry. About before.

"That's all right," Flossie said. She knew that Grace had simply been angry, and she'd had every right to feel that way — her mother and sister had been stripped from her life horribly and needlessly. Flossie was glad to see that Grace seemed calm. Michael had surely had much to do with this, and Flossie was grateful he'd been able to spend time with Grace, keeping her company through her ordeal.

"I don't need to run off anymore," Flossie told Grace. "A lot's happened since I've been gone. Can I tell you what I've been up to?"

Grace's eyes came up from her notebook, which was resting on her lap.

Flossie proceeded to tell Grace all that had happened since she'd last left Lambeth Hospital. About seeing her father. About Viktor Brun. About Elke. About Hana. The telling took some time. As she was finishing up and contemplating how she might try to convince Grace one last time that she should choose to live, a movement behind them in the ward made Grace swivel in her seat.

Immediately, she stood, dropping the twilight notebook and pencil upon the floor.

Flossie stood as well. There was a soldier in the doorway, hovering worriedly, his eyes searching the beds in the ward systematically.

Within seconds, he spotted Grace's living form.

He ran through the ward then — straight toward her. A nurse at the other end of the room told him off loudly, but he paid no attention to her, his eyes fixed upon his target.

Flossie watched him as he approached Grace's bedside. The living Grace's eyes flickered open just in time to see her father round the corner of her hospital bed. Grace reached her hands up, and the pair fell into each other's arms.

Flossie went to say something to Grace's twilight form.

But it was no longer there.

The place she'd sat in was empty, only her twilight notebook and pencil lying on the floor.

Grace had made her decision. She'd returned to her body and awoken herself.

She'd decided to live.

In the hospital bed Grace was sitting up, her arms wrapped tightly around her father's khaki-uniformed back. Grace's eyes opened and searched for the spot where she knew Flossie had been. Their eyes connected, despite the fact that Grace now couldn't see her.

Thank you. Her eyes shone, just as Elke's had. *Thank you.*

Chapter 32

*In which Flossie and her friends
visit St. Paul's*

Grace's mother and sister were buried together at Tower Hamlets a few days later.

As well as the large party of living who attended, there was also a large, unseen party of the dead. Flossie, Ada, and Violet were in attendance. So were Michael, William, and all the other Chelsea Pensioners, in a sea of tricorn hats, white beards, and muted scarlet coats. Hugo Howsham was there, and the other Turnkeys had also been invited—Alice and Matilda from West Norwood and the Turnkeys of Brompton and Abney Park, too. Even the typesetter from Nunhead managed to tear himself away from his "important business," though he spent most of his time taking notes as he studied the headstones inside the cemetery.

Grace and her father held each other tightly during the interment. A woman and a young girl were present, who Flossie presumed were Grace's aunt and cousin. The woman was rather pale and had her arm in a sling, and Flossie guessed this was why she hadn't been able to make it to see Grace and Ruth in the hospital — she'd been injured herself. Flossie could see that there was much love in the family. Grace had even found her voice, which was more than Flossie could have hoped for. While things would never be the same again, she knew Grace would be all right.

The other Turnkeys left after a while, and the Chelsea Pensioners departed for Brompton Cemetery with their Turnkey at the same time. They were going to return to rest. But only, they said, until such time as their services were required again.

Grace's extended family moved toward the gates of the cemetery as well, leaving Grace and her father to pay their respects above the freshly dug graves. Only Flossie, Violet, and Ada remained nearby.

"They'll be well cared for here," Grace said quietly,

her eyes searching the cemetery for something she couldn't see. "I know they will."

Her father cast a doubtful eye around the cemetery. "Do you think so?"

"I know so." Grace's voice was firm. "It might all be wild and overgrown, but the people here mean well. I know they do."

"She knows she can trust you," Flossie told Ada.

That ever-present frown of Ada's crossed her brow. "Yes, well. I try to do my best," she said gruffly.

Flossie and Violet laughed at her grumpy tone. Even Ada's huge stone angel Advisor, standing close behind her, seemed to lose her grim expression for a split second.

"What?" Ada said, crosser still.

"Nothing," Flossie replied. "Just never stop being yourself, Ada."

The three girls watched as Grace and her father began the slow walk back to the cemetery gates.

As she watched them go, Flossie thought of her own father. Despite the distance between them, she somehow felt as close to him as Grace was to her father in this moment.

"Now what?" Ada asked when Grace and her father were out of sight.

"We return to our cemeteries, I suppose," Flossie said. "And carry on."

"And wait for the bombing to start again this evening, you mean," Ada added for her.

"As it always seems to." Violet sighed.

They were suddenly quiet in their little huddle, the noises of the living filling in the silence — cars and trucks, a grave digger and a groundskeeper talking nearby. It was this juxtaposition of the living and the twilight world that got Flossie thinking.

"Will you come with me somewhere this evening?" she asked her friends.

They met outside Highgate and joined hands as darkness was falling in the winter sky, Flossie transporting them to their destination.

"Oh, Flossie," Ada said when she opened her eyes. "How beautiful. Now I see why you come here all the time."

Violet murmured in agreement as she took in the view from the dome of St. Paul's Cathedral. All was still in the sky apart from the bobbing of the silver barrage balloons, dusted with the orange of sunset.

The threesome walked the perimeter of the Golden Gallery, taking in the view and working out where all of the Magnificent Seven lay.

When they returned to the point at which they'd started, Ada stood next to Flossie. "So, this is where it all began."

"This is where you first saw Viktor Brun?" Violet said. "Up here?"

"Yes," Flossie answered them both.

"It must have crossed your mind that we could do the same," Ada continued. "Spy, I mean. If that officer found a way to pass information to the living, I bet we could find another one. We could win this war in no time."

Flossie could barely speak, her secret of combining the keys stuck in her throat. "I'm sure there are other ways. But we can't. This war isn't ours to win." It was as she'd said to Elke at the start of all this. It wasn't their war. Not their fight. "Even if we won this war for the living, they'd only have more. Remember what they called the last one? The war to end all wars? It didn't take them long to start another one, did it?"

No one spoke. They all knew this was true.

"Anyway, I don't have time for spying," Flossie continued with a forced laugh. "I'm very busy. I have the important task of keeping Mrs. Gough happy for all eternity, remember?"

This, at least, lightened the mood. They changed the topic, discussing the "Mrs. Goughs" of their own cemeteries. And as they did, they kept a watchful eye over their cemeteries and an ear out for the first air-raid siren of the evening and for the bombing to begin yet again.

Author's Note

I'm afraid to say that I've been a bit naughty and toyed with history.

The term "Magnificent Seven" wasn't coined until 1981 by the historian Hugh Meller. However, I've borrowed it for the purposes of this book.

Flossie's father's ship, the HMS *Royal Sovereign*, wasn't actually sent to the Battle of Jutland. It was deemed unready for battle and, because of this, didn't go. I have imagined that it went, with Flossie's father aboard, and that it suffered a different fate.

A Luftwaffe bomb destroyed the British Museum Newspaper Repository at Colindale just before our story starts, in 1940. As I wanted Flossie to be able to access the newspapers, I've instead imagined her visiting the Old Newspaper Reading Room at the British Museum in Bloomsbury.

Several early readers have asked me if dogs were really used to rescue people during the Blitz, and they most definitely were. They weren't all fancy breeds, either. One dog, called Rip, was a stray whose Docklands home was bombed out. He was taken in by an air-raid warden and without any special training ended up rescuing more than one hundred people between 1940 and 1941. Many dogs like Rip received Dickin Medals, the animal version of the Victoria Cross. Other animals that received the medal included horses, a cat, and many fearless message-carrying pigeons!

Bibliography

Arnold, Catharine.
Necropolis: London and Its Dead.
London: Simon & Schuster, 2007.

Meller, Hugh, and Brian Parsons.
London Cemeteries:
An Illustrated Guide and Gazetteer.
5th ed., New York: History Press, 2013.

Turpin, John, and Derrick Knight.
The Magnificent Seven:
London's First Landscaped Cemeteries.
Stroud, U.K.: Amberley, 2011.

Acknowledgments

*T*he *Turnkey of Highgate Cemetery* has been a long time in the writing and rewriting (and rewriting), and there is a long list of people I need to thank for their help.

Pats for my literate guinea pigs: Pamela Rushby, Peter Rushby, Lyn Rushby, and Emma Aziz.

Huge thanks to Sue Whiting for digging through the rubble until she found the book buried beneath.

Applause for David Belavy for putting up with 503 drafts (it actually might have been more).

A grin for Allison Tait for listening to my incoherent ramblings.

Writing historical fiction can be rather iceberg-ish. The reader sees only the book on top, but underneath is a gigantic pile of notes propping it up. For help with these, I'd like to thank my researcher, Heather Gammage, as well as the Friends of the Magnificent Seven cemeteries. Particular thanks to Bob Flanagan, chairman and publications officer at the Friends of West Norwood Cemetery; Robert Stephenson, trustee at the Friends of Kensal Green Cemetery; and Dr. Ian Dungavell, chief executive at the Friends of Highgate Cemetery Trust. Another thank-you to Paul Talling of Derelict London as well.

Also, thanks to Toowong Cemetery (my local Victorian cemetery) for inspirational walks, and to the Friends of Toowong Cemetery for caring for it.

And to Claudia, who kept my lap warm while I wrote.